ACROSS THE POND

ACROSS THE POND

Joy McCullough

A
atheneum
Atheneum Books for Young Readers

New York   London   Toronto   Sydney   New Delhi

ATHENEUM BOOKS FOR YOUNG READERS
An imprint of Simon & Schuster Children's Publishing Division
1230 Avenue of the Americas, New York, New York 10020

Text © 2021 by Joy McCullough
Jacket illustration © 2021 by Romina Galotta
Jacket design by Greg Stadynk © 2021 by Simon & Schuster, Inc.

For information about special discounts for bulk purchases, please contact Simon & Schuster Special Sales at 1-866-506-1949 or business@simonandschuster.com.
The Simon & Schuster Speakers Bureau can bring authors to your live event. For more information or to book an event, contact the Simon & Schuster Speakers Bureau at 1-866-248-3049 or visit our website at www.simonspeakers.com.
Interior design by Irene Metaxatos
The text for this book was set in Archer.
Manufactured in the United States of America
0221 FFG
First Edition
10 9 8 7 6 5 4 3 2 1
Library of Congress Cataloging-in-Publication Data
Names: McCullough, Joy, author.
Title: Across the pond / Joy McCullough.
Description: First edition. | New York : Atheneum Books for Young Readers, [2021] | Audience: Ages 10 Up. | Audience: Grades 4–6. | Summary: Moving to a Scottish castle allows seventh-grader Callie to escape friendship problems in San Diego, but finding new friends, even in the birding club an old journal inspires her to join, proves challenging.
Identifiers: LCCN 2020012232 | ISBN 9781534471214 (hardcover) | ISBN 9781534471238 (eBook)
Subjects: CYAC: Moving, Household—Fiction. | Friendship—Fiction. | Family life—Scotland—Fiction. | Castles—Fiction. | Bird watching—Fiction. | Scotland—Fiction.
Classification: LCC PZ7.1.M43412 Acr 2021 | DDC [Fic]—dc23
LC record available at https://lccn.loc.gov/2020012232

FOR MARIÑO, WHO MADE ME FEEL
AT HOME IN A NEW LAND

CHAPTER ONE

Callie pressed her forehead to the thick windowpane and looked out across the rolling hills. She wanted to drink in everything at once—the infinite shades of green, the mossy stone walls along winding paths, the sheep grazing in far-off fields. A draft danced across the back of her neck, but the chill was quickly replaced by a flicker of something Callie hadn't felt in ages. Maybe ever.

Possibility.

At home, her life was small. Small apartment, small people. Making herself smaller and smaller until she almost disappeared.

But here, in an actual castle where everything was

larger than any life she'd ever known, where the grassy fields beyond the window stretched out like an ocean of green, she already felt her world expanding.

She felt her *self* expanding.

Callie wasn't the kind of girl who traveled to Europe, like Kate, who "wintered" in Switzerland, or Imogen, who spent her birthday in Paris. The only place Callie had ever traveled was Phoenix. It was sadly lacking in magical firebirds.

But now here she was. In Scotland. In an actual castle.

Even the exhaustion of the endless travel from San Diego to New York to London to Edinburgh to the village of South Kingsferry couldn't extinguish the new thing bubbling up inside her.

"Hey kiddo," her dad said, peeking his head into the billiards room. "Are you joining us for the rest of the tour?"

Of course she was. Callie wanted to turn over every stone in this fortress of a place, from the servants' quarters to the castle keep, an enormous tower at the castle's center. For hundreds of years, the keep had been a lookout to watch for enemies and take refuge if the worst should happen.

"Where's the moat?" Callie's little brother, Jax, had asked when they first arrived. Their parents had laughed.

It wasn't such a silly question, though. Some of Callie's

daydreams in the months leading up to the trip definitely included moats. But her parents had been here before. To them it was less of a fantasy.

"No moat," Dad said. "Or drawbridge. It wasn't the sort of castle with its own military. Just a family and their servants. And visiting nobles."

Generations upon generations of an old Scottish family named Spence had lived and died in this place, and in between they'd had dreams and fears and great loves and crushing disappointments. Even when the Spence line had dwindled down to only Lady Philippa Whittington-Spence, she'd made sure to keep it a place where a family could build something together, safe from intruders.

"Where'd you run off to?" Mom asked, when Dad appeared with Callie in tow.

"I found her in the billiards room," Dad said.

"Billiards?!" Jax screeched, appearing from behind a massive gold chair. "I wanna see!"

He took off running and Dad sprinted after him.

"What do you think?" Mom asked, staring at the massive portrait of a stern man in a military uniform, hanging over the biggest fireplace Callie had ever seen. "I always felt like this guy was judging me."

"Is it all the same?" Callie asked. "From when you lived here before?

"Pretty much. All your first impressions . . . I bet

they're the same as mine the first time I arrived. Almost twenty years ago now!"

"You're old," Callie said, and Mom laughed.

"What do you think? You okay?"

Callie nodded. She was more than okay. "I guess I can't quite believe this is really happening. I mean . . . we *live* here now."

CHAPTER TWO

Callie hadn't believed her parents when they sat her down with Jax and told them their family had inherited a castle, and how would they feel about moving to Scotland? She'd thought it was a trick. Kind of a mean one, actually, when all Callie wanted in the world was to not be where she was at that moment. When things got bad, she'd asked them to pull her out of school and they'd said no. But they were willing to pull her out of the country?

To them, it was a familiar place, though.

Years earlier, Callie's parents had lived in a cottage on the castle grounds and befriended the owner, Lady

Whittington-Spence. Lady as in nobility, which was apparently still a thing.

After her husband died, the lady of the castle had decided to rent out the cottage by the pond as a way to pay the death taxes she suddenly owed. Callie's parents had been the lucky young grad students who happened upon an ad in the newspaper and followed their curiosity to the Spence grounds.

Callie's American parents thought they had stumbled onto an enchanting little rental for their years at the University of Edinburgh. They had no idea how dear they would become to the grand and lonely lady who occupied the sprawling castle. They definitely had no idea that years later, when her will was read, the solicitors would find the entire property had been left to those two students who had shown her kindness while she mourned her husband.

"I live in a caaaaastle!!!!" Jax whooped, bouncing into view and out again before Dad could snatch him.

Mom sighed. "I'd better help keep that one from climbing the walls. I'm not sure they're all structurally sound."

Jax was wired on airplane snacks and adrenaline. He might never sleep again. But it was a big improvement over the whining and moaning when he'd first found out about the move. He hadn't wanted to leave all his friends and his teams and his school. He'd lived all seven years of his life in San Diego and didn't even want to imagine something different.

He'd also pitched a fit when he found out he could only take to Scotland what he could cram into two suitcases. Shipping everything would have been way too expensive, and just because they were moving into a castle didn't mean they were rich. But what about Jax's basketball and favorite books and video games and folders full of baseball cards? Callie would have gone with only her backpack. It was going to be a new life, and who cared about all the stuff she'd thought she needed to get by when that stuff never really got her anywhere but miserable?

Skinny jeans that were never quite right, never looked the same on her as they did on Imogen, and even when Callie had loved that one flowy top and spent all her saved-up money on it, Collin Marks told her he could see her bra strap, and then she never wore it again.

The tweezers she only bought because Lyla said she needed to pluck her eyebrows, and the eyebrow pencil she bought when Kate said she'd plucked too much.

The diary she thought would be a place to pour all her hopes and worries and messy feelings, but really it was an empty book and every time she saw it sitting on her nightstand, the weight of everything it might contain overwhelmed her.

No, Callie had packed light for Scotland, for a new

life. The moment she found out they were moving, she was ready. But she'd had to wait for months while legal stuff got sorted out in San Diego and Scotland—stuff about school enrollment and apartment leases, and travel visas, and on and on. There were a tense few weeks when Callie's parents weren't sure if the Scottish Tourism Trust would grant them the funds they'd need to renovate the castle into a tourist destination. Without those, there was no way they could afford to make the castle livable, much less somewhere other people would want to visit. Callie had started to think it wouldn't ever really happen. Her hopes had floated up only to be yanked back down again.

"Callie!" Jax appeared again. "Come on! You've got to see!"

Callie followed him to the doorway across from the billiards room. Like the rest of the castle, it was dark and a little musty, but then it had been empty and closed up for months. All that time Callie had been waiting to arrive, the castle had been waiting on them, too. The castle might not be a living thing, exactly, but a place couldn't exist for centuries, sheltering generations, and not become entwined with its inhabitants. Callie could barely breathe. These stone walls had witnessed everything.

They'd witnessed girls like her, probably, who'd been crushed and betrayed, but who'd gotten back up and marched out those massive doors to meet what was next. These stone walls could tell Callie things.

"Look how big this fireplace is!" Jax called. "I can stand up inside!"

The grand room had floor-to-ceiling windows and heavy, swooping curtains; decorative carvings on the ceiling; and a massive fireplace at one end. Callie envisioned the parties that must have taken place in this room—the dancing and music, a fire blazing in the enormous fireplace. Maybe even visiting royalty!

Jax stood inside the fireplace and twirled around, kicking up a mini tornado of dust and knocking loose a chunk of stone.

"Jax!" Callie rushed across the room to haul him out. "Let's stay out of the fireplaces until everything gets checked for safety." But once he was clear of avalanches, she stuck her head inside and looked up the long, dark passageway with a tiny patch of sunlight at the end. "It is cool, though."

Their parents' laughter drifted in from a connected room. Apparently they had given up on catching Jax. Callie pulled her little charge with her, determined not to leave him alone. Who knew what else he might get into? This place was big enough to get lost in, and as annoying as Jax could be, his disappearance would be a bad way to start off their new life.

In a room even grander than the one before, her mom and dad stood together at one of the tall windows, looking out across the grounds. An enormous dining table faced the windows, and Callie could almost picture the old lady eating alone as the castle crumbled around her.

"Do you remember," Dad said, "the first time Lady Whittington-Spence had us over for dinner?"

"Right here in the dining room," Mom giggled. "She served rabbit."

"Rabbit?!" Jax squealed.

"We were managing—" Mom said.

"—until we both looked out this window right here," Dad said, "and saw the lawn covered with rabbits!"

They both exploded in laughter.

"We don't have to eat rabbit here, do we?" Jax whimpered.

Callie shivered, maybe at the prospect of eating rabbits, but also because it was even colder inside than it had been outside. It might have been spring, but it was still colder than the coldest-ever day in San Diego. It felt cold enough to snow, though Mom had said they'd have to wait until the next winter to see snow falling. Until then, Callie would imagine the gentle hills around the castle blanketed in white, the bulbs underneath waiting to burst through like a magic trick.

Lyla's family had invited her to go skiing with them

once, but Callie didn't have any gear, and besides, she would have been stuck on the bunny slopes while Lyla and her sisters whizzed down the black diamonds.

Callie shivered again.

"Look at us, reminiscing while you two freeze," Dad said, pulling himself from his memories. "We should probably finish the tour after we've gotten some shut-eye. The solicitor said everything was exactly as Lady Whittington-Spence left it. So we ought to find bedrooms to suit us upstairs. It sounds like this wing is in the best condition, so we'll set up house here while we renovate the rest."

With the suggestion of shut-eye, Callie's lids grew heavy, her limbs leaden. She'd gone without sleep for too long, too cramped and excited and hopped up on possibility to sleep during the flights. She would hear more about the renovation plans in the morning. Her mom had promised to teach her to use the power tools, which she'd never been allowed to do in Mom's workshop at home.

But right now a bed sounded almost as magical as snow-covered castle grounds—not only because she was bone-tired, but also because she needed to burrow under as many blankets as she could find.

Too wild with adrenaline to feel the cold, Jax went running off in another direction, and Mom ran after him. Callie followed her dad out of the dining room toward a massive staircase that went up, then turned, then turned again. She half expected the staircase to swing around like the ones at Hogwarts, and she took a careful look at another stern portrait to make sure it wasn't moving.

"Right this way, milady," Dad said.

The banister was made of a dark, heavy wood, each post thicker and sturdier than one of her dad's legs. A threadbare carpet ran up the center of the stairs, and Dad tripped on a step that bowed under his weight.

"Watch yourself there." He held out a hand to steady Callie.

At the staircase's first turn, Callie paused and looked down at where they'd come from. Dark wood paneling the same color as the banister covered the walls of the cavernous space below them. Four ornate chairs were gathered around a small table in the center of a flowery rug. Two more chairs sat on opposite sides of another table against the wall. Seating for six, and it wasn't even a room—only the base of the stairs!

The castle was musty and dark now, but it wasn't hard to imagine it a few months down the line, after some elbow grease and determination. Her parents were going to transform this place into a destination people would visit to experience the magic of living in a castle for a few days. It would be a vacation her family could never have afforded. But for Callie it wouldn't be a vacation—it would be home.

At the top of the stairs, a narrow hallway stretched out before them. A chandelier drew Callie's eyes upward, and even in the dim light it was impossible to miss the ceilings covered in intricate carvings.

"Whoa," she said.

Dad opened the first door they came upon, but Callie didn't get a chance to see inside before Dad slammed the door shut. "Note to self," he said. "Mousetraps tomorrow. Maybe a cat."

Callie was determined to see the next room, furry inhabitants or not, so she jumped ahead to open the door herself. It was huge, with a mammoth four-poster bed in the middle of the room. But it also had an overwhelming smell of mold. Callie's chest got tight and she made her own note to self: dig out her inhaler as soon as possible.

"Just needs a good cleaning," Dad said. "Why don't we try the other end of the hall?"

Like in any good fairy tale, the third time was the charm: farther down, they found a room filled with flowery, lavender furniture that had probably been there since Lady Whittington-Spence had been Callie's age. The walls were white with pale lavender flowers—wallpaper, Callie thought, until she ran a hand along the wall. "Is that . . . fabric?"

Dad interrupted his inspection of the room to glance at the wall. "Oh yeah," he said. "Some of the walls are covered in silk. It's probably really dusty."

"I love it." Callie crossed her fingers, hoping that her dad wouldn't find something wrong with this room too.

She never would have picked out lavender flowers for her bedroom in San Diego, but right now they seemed absolutely perfect (if a little dusty). Maybe she was a flowery girl after all. Or thoughtful and poetic. Or super into nature. Anything was possible.

Dad grinned. "All right, then. Make yourself at home. I'll go grab your bags."

Alone in the room, Callie sat on one of two fancy and surprisingly comfortable chairs next to the fireplace. Her room had a fireplace! Every room she'd seen so far had a fireplace, actually. It made sense, since the castle had been around long before electricity, and Scotland was perpetually cold and damp. But this fireplace offered no warmth at the moment; it was as cold and dark as the long hallway outside.

Callie got up and hopped around to keep warm.

On one side of the four-poster bed, there was a dark wood rolltop desk and matching chair. She sank into the chair, or at least she tried to, but it was not a sinking sort of chair. Her discomfort didn't matter at all, though. Not once she'd figured out how to roll up the desk's cover to reveal the contents inside.

It was small, not much bigger than a school desk. It wouldn't even fit a desktop computer, not that the former inhabitant of this room would have had a computer. There were all sorts of interesting cubbyholes and drawers against the back, and centered carefully on the desk was a leather-bound journal.

Callie had a sudden memory of reaching out to touch a dinosaur bone at the natural history museum and getting scolded by her second-grade teacher. But Dad had said to make herself at home. This was not only her home; it was her room.

Her very own room. Callie had shared a room with Jax since he was a baby. At first she loved it—he was a good sleeper and she got to see him all sleep-drunk and sweet in the early mornings. But as she got older, it got a lot less sweet. Her parents had given the kids the larger of the apartment's two bedrooms, and when Callie got old enough to need more privacy, they hung up a curtain to divide the room. It hadn't been enough.

She had longed for her own room, like Imogen and Lyla had. Just a normal room to herself. Now she had a room that was all her own and far from normal.

The door Callie assumed was a closet wasn't even normal—it was ornately carved, magical. She pulled it open to discover it wasn't a closet, but a bathroom. Her room connected to a bathroom, and a massive one at that. She stepped inside and burst into laughter. The bathroom was the size of the room she had shared with Jax. The biggest bathtub she had ever seen was the focal point of the entire room. She could easily stretch out and float in there. Two comfy chairs were tucked into the corner around a small table—in case she wanted to have a tea party in the bathroom? And then of course there were the usual bathroom things: toilet, sink, mirror.

She looked for the door that must lead out to the hallway, but the one other door was to a closet with lots of shelves. Callie popped her head back out into the bedroom. The only way into this bathroom was through her bedroom.

She had her own bathroom.

Callie had never been so disappointed to have an empty bladder.

She floated back into the bedroom and returned to the desk. She lifted the leather-bound journal from its spot of honor. Would she be invading the privacy of whoever left it here if she opened it? Or perhaps it would be empty inside, like all those notebooks Callie had never been able to fill because putting her feelings into words seemed about as possible as learning to fly. Or would she open it to find all the secrets and dreams and dramas of a time gone by?

She opened it to the first page. In careful letters with the occasional ink splotch, the inside cover said *Philippa Spence, 1939.*

"Lady Whittington-Spence," she breathed.

She flipped it open to the middle. Instead of hopes and dreams and drama, she found some sort of list. There were dates and locations and . . . birds? "Short-eared owl," she read. "Whooper swan. Red grouse. Rock . . ." She had no idea how to pronounce "ptarmigan."

She set the bird book down and her eyes drifted to the wall above the desk, where a framed document of some sort hung—a diploma, maybe? *Philippa Spence*, the calligraphed name read. This must have been her bedroom, at least as a child.

On the other side of the bed was a wardrobe that quite possibly led to Narnia or else might come to life and help Callie get dressed in the morning. She opened its doors, which let out a delicious creak, and set her backpack inside. She pulled the inhaler from the side pocket before shutting the wardrobe doors, taking a preventive puff, and setting the inhaler on the bedside table.

As grand as it all was, everything was covered with more dust than Callie had ever seen, and that was saying something. Neither of her parents were particularly thorough housekeepers. But the bed was piled high with blankets and pillows to fight off the persistent chill, and none of the rest of it mattered when Callie noticed the best part. There was a window seat.

She was across the room in seconds, dropping onto

the cushioned bench built into the window and ignoring the dust cloud that arose. She lived in a castle, in a room with a window seat! Next to the threadbare cushion was a massive, leaded window looking out across acres and acres of grass and wildflowers and trees, as far as the eye could see.

No mice or mold or musty smells could change this right here. As though by a wish from a fairy godmother, Callie had been lifted out of the life that had fit her like too-small jeans digging into her waist. She'd never really been into princesses, except for a phase when she was three and wore only thrift-store flower-girl dresses for most of a year. But she would take this happily ever after.

From her window, Callie made out a large pond with a cottage on its shore. That had to be the groundskeeper's cottage, where her parents had lived all those years ago. When she'd gotten a bit of sleep, she'd explore. For now she watched a pair of birds swoop and whirl together over the water, sleek and black and acrobatic.

Right when they seemed like an inseparable pair, one of the birds dove toward the pond while the other broke off and winged its way toward the castle. Directly toward Callie's window.

On the stone ledge outside, the bird landed, its shiny feathers settling into place. The quick, furtive movements of its head might have been charming on another bird, but the sharp, powerful beak on this one made clear it was not to be taken lightly. Callie leaned closer, and the raven stood its ground.

Another quick movement of its head, and though the window was grimy and the light starting to wane, Callie was certain the bird had trained its beady eye directly on her.

Callie didn't look away.

1 September 1939
On a train, heading to the Highlands

Mother gave me this book when we parted, as
though it would make up for the fact that she's
sending me away, or that I can't bring Anne and
Diana with me. As though it would make up for
the fact that we could have all gone away together
as a family, to America like Father suggested,
but Mother persuaded him that we should stay in
Edinburgh. Because it would be fine, she said,
the conflict would be over soon.

    But nothing is fine. Germany's invaded
Poland, Charles could be shipped out any day now,
Father's in London, and now I'm being sent to the
Highlands. Our entire family has been scattered,
because Mother couldn't bear to leave her home. I
guess she got what she wanted after all.

    Mother said it would be jolly, like a holiday.
But Mother wasn't the one herded onto a train
car like so much Highland cattle. She wasn't the
one who had to sit next to a lad who insisted
on wearing his gas mask the entire journey.
Aside from looking frightful, he kept mashing me
in the shoulder with it every time he turned his
head.

At least he was in the first group of children to get off the train.

The few chums I knew from school have gotten off at various stops, and now I am left with only a handful of other children I've never seen in my life. Two girls behind me are coal miners' daughters. Yes, I've been eavesdropping. I rather think in times like these, nobody's taking note of minor sins.

But abandoning one's child is not a minor sin, and even if it is, I'm never going to forgive Mother.

CHAPTER THREE

Callie woke to the chattering of her own teeth.

She had fallen asleep almost instantly, the endless travel catching up to her, and she'd slept too hard to notice the cold in the night. But now, despite the blankets piled high, her nose was nearly numb.

She looked longingly at the fireplace, imagining crackling flames. In stories, the chambermaids always stoked the fires before the princess got up. But who made the room warm enough for the chambermaids to drag themselves out of bed? Nobody, that was who, and Callie was no princess.

There had to be heat in this place. It wasn't the 1700s,

and a noblewoman like Lady Whittington-Spence wouldn't have built her own fires. Would she? Callie just needed to find the thermostat and turn it on. She summoned the same determination she'd always used to plunge into the ocean before it was really warm enough to do so, and hauled herself out of bed. Rather than dig around for her warmest clothes, Callie wrapped herself in as many blankets as she could and emerged from the room.

It was colder in the hall, if that was possible. In fact, there was somehow a draft. Maybe her parents had opened a window, in order to air things out. All the doors along the hallway were shut tight. Callie peeked into a few but didn't find her family. Every room had something enticing her to explore, but the heat situation was her first priority.

In San Diego, all she had to do was stick her head out of her bedroom and she'd know in a second where each family member was. Jax was always bouncing a ball, or laughing with friends, or yelling at video games. Mom was usually muttering to herself, or banging around in the kitchen, or using power tools on the patio. Dad was forever typing, somehow the loudest of them all as his fingers clacked away at the keys. Their apartment had been small enough that if one person sneezed, no matter where they were, the others could always hear.

But Callie didn't hear any sneezing or clanking or typing or laughing. With the castle's thick stone walls, she might not hear them even if they were in the next room.

She headed for the staircase, dragging her blankets with her like a train. Jax was an early riser, and he'd probably forced at least one of their parents to get up with him.

"Mom?" she called from the top of the stairs. "Dad?"

No answer but the echo of her own voice in the cavernous entryway below.

"Jaxy?"

Like magic, an elfin sprite, Jax appeared below, in the entrance to a hallway they hadn't explored the night before. "You're up!" he said. "Finally! Come on!"

Tripping over her blankets, Callie descended the stairs and followed Jax (who was wearing only his thin San Diego Padres pajamas) down the hall and into a bright, cheery room. In addition to the countertops and appliances you'd expect to find in a kitchen, there was a dining table, a fireplace, and a seating area with a couch and two armchairs around an old, boxy television.

Her parents were huddled together, coaxing a tiny flame out of a few logs and some wadded-up newspaper. It was marginally warmer in this room than in the rest of the castle. (At least the small part of it Callie had walked through.)

"Callie's up!" Jax announced.

"Callie-kins!" Dad stood, dusting his hands off on pants already covered with black smudges. "How are your fire-building skills? You were a Girl Scout, right?"

"Um." Girl Scouts had mostly been about dancing around in a cookie costume outside grocery stores. "Is there no actual heat?"

Her parents exchanged glances. "There is," Dad said. "But I'm afraid it's not very . . . effective. Hard to heat such a big space. There are fireplaces all over, though!"

Callie looked skeptically at the tiny flame sputtering under her mother's supervision.

"We'll get some space heaters. And we'll do what Lady Whittington-Spence did—keep to a few rooms most of the time, to avoid having to heat the whole castle."

That explained the combination family room–kitchen. But an entire castle to call home, and they'd be stuck in a few rooms?

Callie's stomach grumbled. "Is there anything to eat?"

"Over here!" Jax sat at the kitchen table, which was covered in the various snack foods that had sustained them on their international journey—granola bars, nuts, beef jerky, crackers.

"I'd hoped to get into town for some groceries before you kids woke up," Mom said, giving up on the pathetic little fire. "But the travel wore me out!"

"That's okay. Now I can go with you."

Callie couldn't wait to see South Kingsferry. The small village right on the water sounded like a storybook setting, from her parents' descriptions. Almost too good to be true. Callie was prepared for a Disney-birthday level of disappointment, but at the same time the castle had been more than she'd ever imagined. Maybe the village would be too. To get their groceries, they'd go to three separate shops: a greengrocer for fruits and vegetables, a butcher for meat, and a dry goods store for packaged foods like cereal and pasta.

Her parents had explained to both Jax and Callie that the food would be different in Scotland, even when they were cooking at home. They wouldn't have to eat rabbit, of course, but they wouldn't see the brands they were used to on the grocery store shelves.

"Maybe we can get some fire starters too," Dad said. "Logs and matches don't seem to be doing the trick."

Mom added them to her list.

Real food, a glimpse of the village, and the promise of heat? Callie grinned. "How soon can we be ready?"

Ten minutes later they were back in the tiny car. It was only slightly less cramped without all the suitcases. Jax still wore his pajamas, but Callie had forced herself out of her sleep shirt and sweatpants (and blanket burrito) and into jeans and a slouchy sweater from the shopping trip her grandma had taken her on to prepare her for a cooler climate. She'd even wrestled her hair into a decent ponytail. It was a small village; she could meet a future classmate, and she didn't want to look like she'd just rolled out of bed (even though she had).

Driving away from the castle this time, she let herself marvel at the beautiful grounds as they made their way along. Even as tiny as the car was, she and Jax could roll down the windows and touch the bushes on either side of the car if they wanted to. Every now and then a protruding branch would whap the window.

"I used to take Lady Whittington-Spence's dog along this lane for a walk to get the mail," Mom said. "A mile to the postbox!"

"And how much farther to the village?" Callie asked.

"About another mile. So that's a four-mile trip there and back. Bit of a walk. But you could bike it."

Callie hadn't ridden a bike in years. But, she supposed, there was a reason they said that thing about riding a bike. She'd learned when she was little, but once it stopped being a thing the neighborhood kids did for fun, she outgrew that first bike and never got another. And she'd never ridden a bike along a bumpy, winding path like this one. She wouldn't particularly want to come face-to-face with a milk truck here!

But maybe the new Callie zipped all over the Scottish countryside on a bike!

Mom turned off the castle lane and onto the main

road. Instead of the dense trees and bushes lining either side, now rolling hills stretched out on both sides, some buildings visible in the distance. On the castle grounds, it felt like they were living in their own world, which was okay with Callie. Now there were signs of other people's lives in this magic place.

Somebody took care of those sheep over there.

Somebody played on the swing hanging from that tree.

Lots of somebodies carried on with their lives aboard the double-decker green bus that rumbled by as they came to an even busier road.

"When can I go to school?" Jax asked. "And find a soccer team?"

"Football," Callie corrected, but Jax ignored her.

"Hold your horses, buddy," Dad said. "Let's start with breakfast. We'll get to all of that. Remember, we're here for good! We've got all the time in the world."

It was a little daunting when he said it that way, but hope bubbled up inside of Callie. She had lived one way her entire life—in a rented apartment in San Diego, going to school with the same kids she'd known since kindergarten, trying to keep Jax from running into traffic while her parents both worked constantly at jobs they hated. And now, with the death of one old lady she'd never met, her whole life had changed.

Her parents had sold everything they owned to get

them here and started on renovating the castle into a tourist destination. They'd even borrowed money from her grandparents, which had been a whole thing. Callie wasn't supposed to know about it, but their apartment was small. It had been impossible to avoid overhearing the arguments.

"You said you never wanted to take their money!" Dad had said.

"I don't! But there's no other way to make this happen," Mom had insisted.

Callie's other grandma was the one person she'd miss from back home. She had no money to offer them, but she had given them everything else since she'd moved to San Diego when Callie was born. She had cared for Callie and then Jax while their parents worked; she had filled their apartment with the smells of snickerdoodles and apple crisp; she had knitted scarves and mittens and hats in preparation for their big move.

Mom turned onto an even busier road, with cars zipping by on both sides. Neighborhoods filled with tidy one-story homes appeared, so many lives unfolding inside them. Then, at the crest of the hill, there was the most gorgeous view.

"The village," Mom sighed.

"Oh, honey," Dad agreed.

"That's it?" Jax said.

It was small, but even from a distance Callie could

see how special it was. Beyond the line of jagged roof-tops, chimneys protruding from each one, still gray water reflected the clouds above. Across the water stretched two massive bridges, reaching the shores on the other side of the wide inlet.

One bridge was bold and red, reminding Callie of San Francisco's Golden Gate Bridge, with three massive arches supported by stone pillars. The other was simpler, more common-looking. Gray cables were strung between tall white posts.

"The bridges!" Jax exclaimed.

"Yep," Dad said. "The Jax bridge and the Callie bridge!"

Mom laughed. "Which one is which?"

"Oh, let's see . . ."

Callie held her breath, her new identity in Scotland suddenly hinging on what Dad would say next.

"I think Jaxy is probably the red one," he said. "Don't you? Flashy and fiery? And Callie's the white. Classic and elegant!"

Callie's heart sank. She wasn't sure she wanted to be flashy and fiery. But classic and elegant really meant bor-ing. She tuned out as Mom went on to explain how the red bridge was for a train and the white bridge for cars.

As they came down the hill toward the village, they passed a bus stop where several girls Callie's age sat laughing and looking at their phones, coats wrapped around them against the cool morning air. Of course she wouldn't run into any kids in the village this morning—they were off to school!

The prospect of school was terrifying, but it also sent more bubbles of hope burbling around in Callie's stomach. She was nervous to be the new kid but secretly hoping she'd be a mirror image to Venetia Charles, a British girl who'd been an instant celebrity when she arrived at Callie's school in fifth grade. Someone from another country is always fascinating, and now that person was Callie.

Callie was jolted out of her fantasy of instant popularity by the literal jolt of the tiny car on cobblestones—they had reached the village.

"I forgot about parking," Mom said. "Spoiled by California parking lots for too many years."

"Over by the church, remember?" Dad said.

The little car turned away from the narrow, twisty path of tightly packed shops and toward a more spacious block with a police station, a post office, and an ancient stone church covered in moss and ivy.

"Is that abandoned?" Callie marveled as they parked next to the church and climbed out of the car.

"I don't think so," Dad said. "Look how clean the stained-glass windows are."

He was right. The green crawling along the walls had

looked out of control at first glance, but it was carefully trimmed back from the windows so the jewel-bright colors could catch the light.

"This way," Mom said, leading them away from the church and toward the row of shops. "This is called the high street."

Not only was the narrow street cobbled, but the sidewalks were a mash-up of stones with moss and grass poking through. Jax immediately hopped up on a low stone wall and walked along it like a balance beam.

"Careful, Jaxy," Dad said. "The moss will make it slippery."

The tallest building on the compact high street was a clock tower, with a base of ancient stone and three more stories dotted with arched windows, climbing up to a striking black-and-white clock, weather vane spinning wildly at the top.

Most of the buildings were two stories, some three, and all tightly packed together. Some had no space between them, but occasionally a narrow alley between buildings offered a glimpse of the water beyond, and sometimes the bright red bridge. The Jax bridge.

"Oh look, the butcher!" Mom squealed. "Just like before!"

Callie wrinkled her nose at the slabs of meat hanging in the window.

"Wasn't the dry goods store right next to the butcher?" Dad asked.

"Hmm, I thought so." Next to the butcher was a real estate office instead.

The heavy gray clouds rumbled, but they were no match for the brightly colored awnings on the shops and the row of cheery houses across the way, each one loaded with flower boxes.

Mom stopped the first person to pass by, and Callie cringed as she always did when Mom made instant best friends with strangers. To make things more cringey, this girl was young and edgy-looking, with a nose ring and short, buzzed hair. "Excuse me," Mom said. "But what's happened to the dry goods store?"

The girl stopped and tugged earbuds out. "Sorry, what?"

Mom repeated the question while Callie shrank behind her dad.

"The dry goods store? It used to be right next to the butcher?"

The girl gave a hesitant smile. "You need groceries? There's a Tesco a bit up the road thataway." Her accent was strong, and Callie loved the way her mouth curled around the words. The girl waited for a second, then put her earbuds back in and went on her way. "Good luck," she called over her shoulder.

"Tesco?" Mom repeated.

"Sounds like a gas station," Jax said.

"It's a supermarket chain," Dad said.

Jax hopped off the wall and went running across the cobblestones to a bright red telephone booth. He shut himself inside and made faces at them through the cloudy glass.

"I thought those were only in movies," Callie said. The whole thing felt like a movie set, really.

"Probably soon they will be," Dad said. "Everyone with their own phones now. But I remember calling your mother from that very phone when I'd had one too many pints at the pub and needed a lift back to the castle."

"Peter!" Mom scolded, as though Callie didn't know her dad enjoyed a beer every now and then.

"Should we find the Tesco?" Dad said.

Callie trailed her hand along the iron spikes of a little fence lining the sidewalk until she came to a lamppost straight out of Narnia. A supermarket chain might not be as charming as a greengrocer and a butcher and a dry goods store, but maybe there was a better chance Callie would find some familiar food in a bigger grocery store, and her stomach was starting to growl.

It turned out the greengrocer still existed, but the dry goods store had gone out of business a decade earlier when the supermarket came to town. Callie's parents learned all this and more because they chatted with every single person they passed. Roaming the aisles of the Tesco, they found some familiar things—produce, milk, chicken—and some unfamiliar things, like oatcakes, black pudding (which was *not* a dessert), and something called digestive biscuits, which Mom was way too excited about, considering they sounded like food for an upset stomach.

When they were finally done—in other words, there was no one left in the store to interrogate—Callie was eager to get the bags of groceries back to the castle. She was starving, and also her parents needed to chill with the socializing. But on their way to the car, she spotted something.

"Is that a library?"

Her parents grinned at each other. "We can't stay too long, what with the milk and eggs," Mom said. "But we can check it out."

This time Callie was the one who took off without waiting for the rest of her family members. She trotted half a block back toward the high street and was up the steps of the red brick building in a flash. There would be nothing unfamiliar here. Books were books were books. But Callie's heart sank when she went through the doors and realized the South Kingsferry Public Library was no bigger than her English classroom back home.

"Morning! Can I help you?"

Seated at the checkout desk was a young black woman with sparkly glasses, a blouse covered in tiny books, and an explosion of curls, some of which were blue, purple, and pink.

"Um, hi."

The woman smiled. "I haven't seen you in here before. Are you visiting?"

Callie took a couple more steps inside. "We just moved here. Into Spence Castle?"

"Oh! The Americans, aye?" The librarian stood and came around the desk, holding her hand out to shake Callie's. "Welcome! I'm Esme, and this is the South Kingsferry Public Library."

"I'm Calliope." Her full name surprised her, a delicacy she'd turned her nose up at back home, but now she tasted it anew. In this place, could she be a girl who lived up to a name like Calliope?

"Calliope, lovely. Fancy a tour?"

A tour didn't really seem necessary, considering the size of the place, but before Callie could say anything, Jax burst through the door behind her, followed by their parents.

"This place is small," Jax announced.

Esme laughed, loud enough that the school librarian in San Diego would have shushed her. "Hello to you, too, laddie. There's more than meets the eye here. Don't judge a book by its cover and all that."

After introductions had been made all around, Callie's parents drifted over to a notice board filled with news about town events.

"Right, then, how about that tour?" Esme didn't wait for Callie or Jax to answer. She marched toward the back of the room, so Callie followed, realizing halfway there that stairs led up and down from the main floor. "This floor's mainly our adult fiction, periodicals, DVDs, and computers." She pointed to each area as she said them. "But let's get to the good stuff."

Esme headed down first, and Jax was right behind her. Callie followed. She knew she'd be back no matter what she found upstairs or down, because even if she reinvented herself, she'd never stop reading. (And also, if she was honest, Esme was totally intriguing.)

"This is still boring," Jax said when they reached the bottom.

Esme laughed again, but more quietly, since a man sat nearby, hunched over a table surrounded by books. "Excuse me, young sir," she said, "but are military tanks boring? Or velociraptors? Or video-game design? Because you can find books on all those things down here in the nonfiction and reference section."

She grinned at Jax's hungry expression and waved

them along into another room. Chairs were stacked against the wall, there was a piano in the corner, and posters of celebrities encouraging reading lined the walls. It looked exactly like the story-time room from home.

"This is our meeting room," she told them.

"We're too old for story time," Jax said.

She shrugged. "Oh, I don't know. I think no one's too old for story time. But very well. We have all sorts of other things going on here. Book clubs, yoga classes, Minecraft workshops"—she acted like she didn't hear Jax's yelp—"but I'm sure that would be of no interest to you. Follow me, then."

They tiptoed past the man at the table and over to the staircase, where Esme led them back up to the main floor and then to the floor above it. Over her shoulder she whispered, "Best for last."

When Callie reached the top of the stairs, she let out a yelp of her own. The upstairs was an attic space, with sloped ceilings and stained-glass windows at each end. The edges of the room where the roof sloped down too low to stand were lined with beanbags and cushions and plush couches. It was heaven.

"Picture books at this end," Esme pointed out. "Books for teens at that end. Middle readers in the middle, as one might expect. It's all a bit heavin', but we make it work."

Jax bolted for the middle.

"This is amazing," Callie said. "What's 'heavin''?"

"Ah, sorry," Esme said. "Crowded. But if you're going to be crowded by something, I think books are ideal, don't you?"

"Callie? Jax?" Dad poked his head up into the upper level. "We've really got to get back with the groceries."

Jax rushed at him. "You have to stay downstairs," he said. "This floor is kids only."

Esme coughed over a laugh. "Oh, no. As long as you love the books up here, you're welcome. After all, this is my favorite section of the library!"

"Thanks for the tour," Callie said. "I'll come back soon. I finished the only book I brought on the plane."

Esme's eyebrows shot up. "You head on down. I'll be right behind you."

By the time they'd regrouped on the main floor, Esme was tripping down the stairs, waving a book. She pressed it into Callie's hands. "Take this one," she said. "So you'll have something to read until next time."

"I'm afraid we don't have time to get all set up with a card," Mom said.

Esme waved her concern away. "That's all right. I trust you. And I know where to find you. Spence Castle, right? Welcome to South Kingsferry."

Callie hugged the book to her chest, thanking Esme

and scurrying to catch up with her family. "I'll be back," she said.

"I know you will!"

Outside, Callie looked at the book. *Goodbye Stranger* by Rebecca Stead. Now there was at least one person in South Kingsferry who didn't feel like a stranger at all.

CHAPTER FOUR

A castle, Callie learned over the next few days, was not at all the same thing as a palace.

That didn't mean the castle wasn't incredibly cool. It absolutely was. The enormous windows and high ceilings, the grand staircase and all the fireplaces, the turrets and battlements. There was an elevator that opened by pulling on an extremely heavy iron grate, though no one could figure out how to make it move up and down. There were even these holes above the castle's entryway called murder holes, which Dad explained were used to pour boiling oil on intruders or shoot arrows at them.

But the mice Callie and Dad had seen on the first

night were only the beginning of the hazards.

Lots of the wood in the grand staircase was rotted through, making the climb up or down a rather perilous journey. Another huge chunk of stone fell right next to Jax as he explored one of the enormous fireplaces. A string of rainy days had been very useful for identifying the many places the roof leaked. And mice weren't the only creatures in the castle.

Jax thought every new calamity they discovered was the coolest thing ever, including the falling chunk of stone that could have killed him. But Callie found that each mounting problem popped a tiny bubble of her hopes. Her parents had been poor and stressed in a tiny apartment back home. Now they were poor and stressed in a massive castle. Only their circumstances had changed; they were still the same.

When the hazards in the rest of the castle overwhelmed her, Callie retreated to her lavender room with the window seat. Here, the new surroundings made her feel like a completely different person. Once she'd taken care of the dust situation and aired out the bed linens, the room had become even more magical. She hoped that with work and time, the rest of the castle would follow.

Her parents kept saying things with forced cheer like, "Well, we knew it would be a lot of work!" and "Well, you get what you pay for, ha ha ha!" and "Well, we do love a challenge!"

The addition of space heaters to their bedrooms and main living spaces was helping, and one morning about a week after they'd arrived, Callie found she could peek her head out from under the covers without chattering teeth. Mom had promised they could work together that morning to make a list of the most pressing renovation projects and start setting up a workshop in the old stables. That was motivation enough to get out of bed, no matter how chilly.

When Callie reached the kitchen–family room, it was warm enough to drop her blanket burrito on the couch. A decent fire burned in the fireplace, and Dad stood at the stove, scrambling eggs.

"How'd you sleep, Callie-kins?"

She rubbed the grit from the corners of her eyes. "There was a weird sound coming from my chimney."

"Ghosts!" Jax shouted, swooping around the room, flapping his arms more like a bat than a ghost. That was normal. What was weird was that he was completely dressed. Jax never got dressed until the very last minute before they had to leave the house.

"Where's Mom?"

"Right here," Mom said from behind Callie. She was fully dressed too, which was even weirder.

"What is happening?" Callie sank into a kitchen chair.

"I'm going to school!"

"What?"

"Jax and I are heading down to the primary school to enroll him," Mom said. "Later, you and I will go to the secondary school."

Callie's stomach turned, and she pushed the scrambled eggs around the plate. "Already?"

"Well, it's the middle of the semester. Or term, they say. Might as well get in there sooner than later. Be ready around noon?"

Then Mom and Jax were gone, and Callie had lost her appetite.

"I thought I'd have a little more time to adjust," she said as the car bounced along the cobblestones in the village. She hated the whine in her voice—the new Callie wasn't a whiner—but she'd barely gotten over the jet lag and now she was supposed to enroll in school?

"Adjusting to living in the castle is one thing," Mom said. "But you're not going to adjust to the new culture until you're around people other than us."

Callie sighed.

"I don't understand," Mom went on. "I thought you were excited to make new friends."

She had been. Though now that she thought about it, really she was excited to *have* new friends. The part where she had to make them was suddenly very daunting. But she reminded herself of Venetia Charles back in fifth grade. Callie would be the new girl this time. The new *American* girl. She would be interesting. Not only interesting—*fascinating*. She'd have her pick of friends.

Then her mother pulled the car into the driveway of a red-roofed institutional building with a sign that said SOUTH KINGSFERRY HIGH SCHOOL.

"Wait, high school?"

"Take a breath, hon." Mom pulled into a parking spot. "They don't have middle school here. It's primary school, then high school. You'll be in what they call Second Year. But it's twelve- and thirteen-year-olds. Exactly like seventh grade back home."

Callie's heart pounded. High school? Being the interesting new American at a middle school was one thing. She was not ready for high school. In any country.

When Callie made no move to get out of the car, her mom squeezed her hand. "You're not starting classes today. Let's go on in, do the paperwork, and give it a looksee."

That was easy for Mom to say. But Callie didn't have a lot of options. She climbed out of the car, shoved her hands in her hoodie's pocket, and followed Mom to the school's entrance.

Outside and in, the building looked pretty much like

any school anywhere. But right as they stepped inside, the bell sounded for a passing period and the halls flooded with students. The first thing Callie noticed was the uniforms.

"I thought this was a public school," she said. Living in a castle sounded fancy, but Callie's parents were spending every cent they had to make all the repairs. They definitely could not afford private school.

"It's called a comprehensive school," her mom said. "It's basically the same as an American public school."

All around, students laughed and shouted and buried heads in their phones, all wearing navy blazers and crisp white shirts, with neckties on the boys and girls. Some girls wore plaid skirts and some wore the same navy trousers as the boys.

"But the uniforms . . ."

"Oh. Yes! Won't it be nice not to have to worry about what to wear?"

Callie actually didn't hate that idea. No squeezing herself into skinny jeans or saving all her money to buy a top that was suddenly out of style the moment she wore it.

"Here's the office." Mom pushed through a glass door and Callie was glad to escape inside, where she could watch the students passing by like fish in an aquarium, rather than getting carried along by the current. Or drowned.

Mom spoke to the receptionist in the background, but Callie kept her attention on the current of students, as if by observation she might spot someone who looked like friend potential. They all looked impossibly old. Like those high schoolers at the bonfire on the beach.

"Callie Feldmeth," her mother said to the receptionist, and then began to spell it.

"Calliope, actually," Callie interjected, trying to ignore Mom's look of surprise.

"The muse of epic poetry," the receptionist said with a smile, making a note on the paperwork.

"Um, yeah."

Callie drifted back to the glass as her mother and the woman discussed boring details. All those boys in ties looked even older than high school. Like college age or something.

"Looking at her schedule from her previous school, we can match her up in largely comparable classes. Algebra, literature, Spanish, Science 1. Social Subjects corresponds to her American history course. Phys ed. If she'd like to do any extracurricular activities, I'm afraid some of those are full. But I believe there's room in marching band. Do you play an instrument, love?"

"Callie?"

She turned to see her mother and the woman across the desk looking expectantly at her.

"She doesn't play an instrument," Mom finally said.

"Well . . . there's room in the finance club."

Callie made a face her mom pretended not to see, but the woman laughed.

"Don't blame you, love. But there's only a few more months in the term, and then you'll have the same chance as everyone at whatever interests you. Not to mention, once you're at university and beyond, finance will serve you a fair bit better than the clarinet."

Callie zoned out to listen while the woman went over the uniform requirements and other school policies. Now she was thinking about finances and being responsible for her own money once she was in college. Her parents had never had a lot, but at least they'd had Mom's family to fall back on. What if Callie needed help? But she shouldn't have to think about things like paying rent yet. She was only in seventh grade. Or Second Year, as they said here. Why did everything after elementary school feel like a Slinky going down stairs faster and faster until it finally ended up in a tangled heap?

"Right, then, how about we show you around the place?"

"That would be great," Callie's mom said, poking her in the ribs with her elbow.

The woman leaned back and hollered toward an open doorway. "Rajesh, love! Come here, would you?"

A small, black-haired boy with warm dark skin appeared, wearing the same uniform as the other students, except it looked enormous on him, like he was wearing his dad's suit. Finally, someone who actually looked younger than Callie. "Yes, miss?"

"This is Calliope. She's new. Would you show her the highlights of our fair institution?"

Rajesh nodded gravely at the secretary. "I will give it my all, Miss Clark." He grinned at Callie with a twinkle in his dark eyes.

"Brilliant!" Miss Clark beamed at him. "Miss Feldmeth, your mum and I will stay here and do a bit more paperwork while you two have all the fun."

Rajesh opened the door to the now-quiet hallway and held it for Callie. "The highlights of our fair institution," he said, "include golf trophies"—he made game-show arms at a mostly empty display case of tarnished trophies—"cringe-worthy productions of plays by old white guys"—he waved his arm at the sign pointing toward the auditorium—"and aggressively mediocre cafeteria food. Shame you're not here on a Tuesday, though."

"Why?"

"Taco Tuesdays. You really haven't lived until you've tried the South Kingsferry High School's appropriation of a traditional Mexican food.

"I'm not Mexican," he added. "But I am a connoisseur

of actual Mexican food. I went with my dad on a business trip to Mexico City last year, and the food was amazing."

"Oh," Callie said. She'd always enjoyed the Mexican food in San Diego, but now she wondered how authentic it was. It was geographically a lot closer to Mexico than Scotland, so maybe that made a difference.

"You're American?" Rajesh said.

"Yeah, um. California?"

"Like Hollywood?"

"A couple hours away."

"Ever see any stars?"

Callie paused. "Sure. At the beach you can see the most, because there are no streetlights there."

Rajesh looked confused but didn't say anything.

"Wait." Callie felt her cheeks grow warm. "You meant like Hollywood stars."

Rajesh grinned. "Yep. Like James Corden! Every awkward musical-theater kid's hero! Ever seen him?"

"No. Are you into musical theater?" Callie could see it. Rajesh was small, but his personality filled the massive hallway.

But at the question, his light dimmed a little. "Not really," he said.

Callie kept her answers to the rest of Rajesh's questions extremely short as he walked her through the school, pointing out the cafeteria, the gymnasium, the auditorium.

It was a school, not especially different from any other school, aside from the uniforms.

"Oi, Raj!" a voice called from an open classroom door. A teacher appeared, nearly as young as the students. The only thing setting him apart was his non-uniform clothes. "If you want that extra credit, you need to hand me those problems by the end of the day." The young teacher blinked at Callie. "Who's this, then?"

"Calliope," Rajesh said. "New-student tour."

"Maybe," Callie said. "We're still deciding."

"Well, come on in! Let's help you make up your mind!"

The young teacher swept an arm toward his classroom, and even though it was the last thing in the world she wanted to do, Callie walked in. She instantly felt like the world's biggest schlub in her jeans and hoodie, in front of this room full of boys and girls in ties and blazers. They were going to take one look at her and know she could never be anyone new, anyone *fascinating*.

But it turned out they weren't paying her much attention.

"Oi, it's Raj!" one of the boys crowed. An enormous one who looked like he'd be a beater on a Quidditch team. "What's up, little fella?"

Raj did a funny little boxing move, like he was ready to spar, but one actual punch from this guy would have knocked Raj out for the count.

A couple of girls toward the back giggled, and one of them waved at Raj.

"Listen up, ladies and gents," said the teacher. "This here is Calliope. She might be coming to our school soon. American by the sound of it, yeah?"

Callie nodded, leaving California out of it. Suddenly her full name sounded absurd, like it belonged to a totally different person. She was a fraud.

"Whereabouts you living now?"

"Here," Callie said. Someone snickered, and the teacher frowned. "I mean, in the castle. The castle by the . . ." She looked around the room, as though she could determine which way to point, as though she had any idea which direction the castle even was, as though any direction mattered besides down, where she wished the floor would open up and swallow her.

"Spence Castle," Rajesh supplied.

A murmur went through the students.

"Is that so? Are you lot related to the Spence clan then?"

"I don't think so?" Callie said, and this time a couple of people snickered. "I mean, no. We're not. My parents, they knew the lady . . . who died . . ."

"Miss Clark's expecting us back in the office," Rajesh interrupted, saving Callie from further embarrassment. "More paperwork."

"Right, then, off you go. Nice to meet you, Calliope of Spence Castle. Raj, I'll have those problems by the final bell, yeah?"

Callie barely made it to the car before the wave of nausea hit. She slammed the door shut, enclosing herself in at least the illusion of safety. She'd left without saying a word to Raj, who probably thought she was a total nutcase. She hadn't even stopped into the main office again. Her mom would figure it out.

All those eyes looking at her, her complete inability to form sentences, the snickers . . .

"Callie?" Mom opened the door. "What happened? That nice boy said you bolted out the front doors."

Callie shook her head. She couldn't speak.

Her mother sighed. "You're on the driver's side."

Callie hadn't even noticed the steering wheel when she got in; she'd tumbled into the car on the normal side and closed her eyes against the oncoming panic.

It would have been much easier to get out of the tiny car and walk around, but Callie couldn't bear the thought of leaving the bubble of safety. She awkwardly crawled over the emergency brake onto the passenger side, then pulled her knees up to her chest and ignored her mother's running monologue of the wonders of South Kingsferry High School all the way home.

1 September STILL
Somewhere outside Inverness

When we reached Inverness, we remaining
evacuees were hustled off the train and
shepherded into the small stationmaster's office.
I expected we would be split off into our various
host homes, but instead we were retrieved and
packed into a minibus, which took us to a
country estate barely deserving of the name. It
was simply a house on decent acreage. Not a very
large house at that.

   We were greeted by a woman I assumed
was the housekeeper. She went over a list of
rules and chores and oh-poor-dears, which I
interrupted to ask when we would be meeting our
hosts. She looked at me like I was quite dim.

   "SHE'S our host," one of the coal miners'
daughters said, and not helpfully, but rather like
she was trying to point out my foolishness.
Which seems to have worked, as the other girls
all burst into giggles.

   I don't care. Despite what Mother said, this
is not a holiday and I am not here to make new
chums. When we are returned to our homes, I will
never see any of these horrid people again.

This is how small the house is: the entire upstairs consists of two bedrooms and a washroom. Two bedrooms! One of those belongs to Mrs Miller, who is apparently our host, though she might have taken off her greasy apron if she didn't want to be mistaken for a housekeeper. That leaves only one other bedroom.

For all five of us evacuees!!!

It's almost as big as my room at home, but that's not nearly large enough for five girls! And there's only one proper bed, which was claimed by the first girl through the door—the one who corrected me—leaving the rest of us to cots!

I know I sound like a horrid brat, and Mrs Miller is doing us a kindness by taking us in. I shall endeavour to rise above these circumstances and save all my ire for Mother, whose fault this is. (And perhaps also Hitler.)

We, the residents of this one room, include the two coal miners' daughters: Magda, who claimed the bed, and June, both around my age. Two smaller girls named Bea and Rosie, who are definitely sisters on account of being identical with their freckles and strawberry-blond curls. And myself.

Mrs Miller told us to run off and explore the

grounds together after being cooped up in the train all day. But I pleaded a headache and was given a reprieve. I'm not sure how often I'll get away with that. Mrs Miller has no children of her own, and I rather think she plans to make up for all the child-rearing she's never done by mothering us all to death.

And to think, we were sent here to be kept safe from threat!

CHAPTER FIVE

"Callie-kins," Dad said, "we're going to be busy renovating the castle. We won't have time to homeschool you."

Callie coughed at the dust billowing from the shelves she was cleaning in the room her parents had designated as the renovation office. All around her, she'd stacked the ancient books that had been on the shelves, but now she couldn't take two steps without tripping over Homer or Robert Louis Stevenson.

"It's not like you have to teach me the alphabet," she said. "Aunt Claire barely does anything with Aidan and Olivia." Her cousins had been homeschooled their whole lives, doing cool projects and reading for hours a day and never once having to play dodgeball. "There are tons of online curriculum options," she said. "And the library in town. I'll work so hard, I promise."

Dad sighed, wiping the room's grimy windows. He hadn't immediately objected. There was a reason she'd asked him first.

"Plus, if I'm homeschooled, I'll be around to help out more!" Callie said, sensing an opening. "Couldn't we try it for the rest of this semester? It's only a couple of months. And if I don't keep up with lessons, I can enroll at the school in the fall. Please?"

"I'll talk to Mom," he finally said. "But won't you be lonely?"

Searching for Jax on the castle grounds, Callie couldn't imagine ever being lonely. There was too much to explore. The estate went on forever, winding paths and rolling fields. Callie had never seen grass so green—it was over-grown, but the lush emerald carpet made her want to lie down and make a grass angel.

Fantasies about being the intriguing new girl were simply that—fantasies. But this, here, was real. Lasting. The enormous trees were bigger than anything she'd ever seen before, epic beasts that had probably been there for hundreds of years. Wildflowers were starting to bloom. All around a gnarly, sideways tree that seemed to have fallen over and taken root where it lay, cheery daffodils made a carpet of bright yellow.

Finally Callie reached the pond and looked across to the little cottage on the opposite shore. She made her way along the path around the water. From her bedroom window, the cottage had seemed closer. But as she got near, it looked more magical. Like so many other things, it was made of mossy, cobbled stone. Almost definitely home, at one point if not now, to a witch or an elfin queen.

The only thing was, Callie was starting to realize she and Jax should have made some clearer boundaries for their game of hide-and-seek. She had reached the opposite side of the pond, and there were still an infinite number of places her brother could be hiding.

"Jaxy! I give up!"

No response but some ravens croaking overhead.

It was just as well. Jax got mad when she found him too quickly, and this way she got some time to explore, plus credit for keeping Jax out of her parents' hair. She'd be worried about getting lost on the sprawling grounds, except that so far, no matter where she went, she could still catch a glimpse of the castle's keep, the tall tower connecting the two large sections of the castle.

She'd refused to talk to her parents about what had happened at the school. Mostly because she couldn't really say. Some kids had snickered? But it had been so much more than that. It had been the crushing realization that all her dreams of reinvention had been absurd. A school was a school and hierarchies of kids were the same everywhere and she would never fit.

She wasn't going back there. Mom had said they could "think about it" for a few days, which meant go back and officially enroll unless Callie could come up with another plan. She already had the plan—her job now was to get her parents to agree to it.

She'd asked to be homeschooled back in San Diego. After everything happened. Her parents had said no. They were way too busy with their jobs, and what about college, and she'd miss all her friends. They didn't know what a joke that last part was. She'd started researching how to make it work, but then they'd gotten the news about how her parents had inherited a Scottish castle and all plans went out the window.

Now it could really happen.

Callie rounded the cottage to reach the edge of the pond. Ducks floated on the glassy surface. But instead of being struck by the peacefulness of it all, a sick feeling turned over in her stomach.

Jax couldn't swim. As athletic as he was in all other things, they had tried to enroll him in swimming lessons multiple times, to great consternation.

"Jaxy?" Callie called.

She didn't really believe her brother was lying at the bottom of the pond. Surely the ducks wouldn't be so calm if a child had just thrashed his way under the water. And she would have heard a splash—wouldn't she?

Callie picked up a rock and tossed it as far into the pond as she could, if only to hear something besides her pounding heart. The rock landed with a satisfying *plonk*. She whirled around at the crack of a stick nearby and scanned the trees. No sign of Jax.

Then the curtains fluttered in the little cottage where her parents had lived as grad students. The overgrown weeds all around the cottage and the ancient bicycle propped up beside it suddenly made the whole thing less charming and way creepy. The curtain's movement was nothing, probably, or at least something with an obvious explanation. Like the spooky sounds coming from her chimney at night.

"Boo!"

Callie jumped and screamed and Jax collapsed in fits of giggles.

"Not funny, Jaxy!"

"Totally funny."

He was laughing so hard he snorted, which only made him laugh harder. It was all so easy for Jax. He made instant friends wherever he went. He probably loved standing in front of a new classroom and giving everyone the chance to line up and be his buddy. If Callie was going to reinvent herself as someone, she should probably try to be more like Jax than Venetia Charles.

She plopped down on the grass next to him and mussed his hair. "I think we've got to make some ground rules for hide-and-seek, little bro."

At dinner that night—which included chicken breasts her parents had to swear to Jax were not rabbit meat—Callie kept expecting them to bring up homeschooling, but every time a new subject came up, it was something completely uninteresting. The great landscaper they'd found to work on the grounds, the permits involved in making the castle keep safe for visitors, the pros and cons of allowing developers to put a golf course on the land to the east of the castle.

Finally, after Callie had cleared most of the dishes and Dad had set the water on to boil for tea, he cleared his throat in the familiar way that meant he was about to say something momentous.

"Your mother and I have been talking," he said, "about homeschooling."

"Homeschooling?!" Jax, still lingering over his green beans, clattered his fork onto his plate. "But I want to go to the primary school!"

"We know." Mom placed a calming hand on his shoulder. "This is about Callie."

Jax's head whipped to Callie, but Dad spoke again before Jax could interrogate her.

"We've decided to try it, if you're sure it's what you want—with a few conditions."

Callie's heart surged. "Anything."

Mom gave Dad a look that didn't bode super well, but Callie was serious. She would do anything not to be the schlubby weirdo in a school full of strangers with their sophisticated accents and pristine uniforms and finance clubs.

"First, you have a week to make a plan that addresses what you'll be doing for writing, math, science, and history. Second, we'll have weekly check-ins. If you are not keeping up with your learning to our satisfaction—"

"My satisfaction," Mom interjected.

"—to Mom's satisfaction, you will be enrolling in South Kingsferry High in the fall. The main reason we're willing to try this is because there are only a couple of months left in the semester, as you pointed out. We don't want you to do this because you're afraid to meet new people. We know you went through a difficult time with your friends back home—"

Callie opened her mouth to object, but Dad held up his hand and kept talking. "That's why our final condition is this: you must find a social activity in which you will inter- act with young people your age. Regularly."

Callie's heart plummeted back down. How was she supposed to do that?

"You should do soccer with me!" Jax said. "I mean, not on my team, probably, because I'm way better than you, but I bet they have a beginner team."

"You'll be ready to tell us about the activity when you tell us the rest of the plan. In a week."

Callie spent the next several days fluctuating wildly between the joy of finally being able to try home-schooling and terror that she'd be thwarted by the social requirement. She had her academic plan ready almost right away, having thought about it for months already. She'd keep a daily journal and read through an ambitious list of books. She'd found online curriculums for math and science. And for history and writing, she was going to study all the real events in the *Hamilton* musical and write a research paper. There was no way her parents would object to any of it.

But a social activity? In the tiny village of South Kingsferry? She didn't even know how to go about that. She did some half-hearted searching online, but when she didn't really have defined interests like Jax did with all his sports, it was hard to know where to begin.

She definitely did not want to play soccer, or football as they called it here. She was a terrible player, as Jax had pointed out, and sports could only lead to more humiliation.

There might be something like Girl Scouts here, but she hadn't really loved that in the States, either. Anything involving a performance was a clear no. An orchestra, a theater troupe, a dance class—no, no, and no.

All Callie really loved was reading. Somehow she didn't think her parents would consider going to the South Kingsferry Public Library to be a social activity. Although it could be a good place to start. Maybe they'd have a kids' book club or something.

She tried her dad first, but he couldn't take her into town because he was meeting with the new landscaper to discuss the plans for the grounds. She wandered out the grand front entrance and headed over to the stables, through the arched doorway at the far end of the castle and into a courtyard with a fountain in the middle. The six doors to the stables were thrown wide, and inside, Mom was in her element, sawing planks of wood.

Callie had expected to find hay and saddles the first time they opened up the stables, but they hadn't been used for horses since Lady Whittington-Spence was a child. When Callie's parents had lived in the cottage, the stables had been filled with the late Lord Whittington's fancy automobiles. His widow had sold them off one by one as her fortune dwindled, and now it was a wide-open space perfect for her mom's power tools and the giant mess they always made.

"I'm trying to get all the wood cut today to replace the rotted stairs," Mom said. "I want to get that done before we get the electrician in. I can't spare any time."

"How am I supposed to find a social activity if I can't get to town?" Callie asked.

"Beats me, hon." Mom flipped her safety visor down. "You could walk. It's up to you to make this work." Then she turned her power saw back on and the conversation was over.

It was totally unfair. If she were going to school, her parents would be driving her back and forth every day. Now she was on her own to fulfill their dumb requirement? Unfair or not, Callie was determined to make it happen. Anything was better than South Kingsferry High School.

Four miles wasn't exactly a marathon, but it was about as far as Callie had ever walked at one time. She wandered into the courtyard outside the stables. The fountain was dried up and probably hadn't run in years. Against one of the courtyard walls stood a marble statue of three girls in an embrace. From the look of their drapey robes, they were from mythology, but Callie couldn't place them. She could find out who they were if she could make it to the library.

But walking there and back before dark seemed unlikely, and mostly she didn't want to walk that far. Bike, maybe. But walk . . .

That was when she remembered the ancient bike she'd seen propped up by the cottage.

CHAPTER SIX

Callie wobbled a bit as she got used to the bike, and she wasn't helped much by the fact that the brakes didn't work and the path wasn't smooth. Eventually she called on muscle memory and built her confidence, remembering that the ride would be smoother if she pedaled faster. Soon bright pink and red flowers whizzed past in a blur as she flew down the lane.

She'd never admit it to her parents, but this was amazing. Her hair whipped around her face and her heart flipped into her throat. She was totally free. She could go anywhere. No one's eyes were on her. It wouldn't surprise her if the bike lifted up off the ground and she started pedaling through the sky!

But then she truly was airborne, flying into a bush.

As she assessed her limbs for damage beyond that to her dignity, Callie was grateful that at least no one had witnessed her humiliation, except for some plump birds she'd been seeing everywhere and kept meaning to ask her parents about. She climbed out of the flowering bush and picked the leaves from her hair. This was a setback, but the bike still worked. Nothing was broken. Callie righted the bike and set off again, trying to pedal confidently but not so wildly that she had another collision.

Once she got the feel for the bike, the two miles from Spence Castle to the village of South Kingsferry flew by like nothing. Aside from the lack of brakes, it was in decent working condition. Which was weird, considering how long it had probably been standing there, next to the cottage, exposed to the rain and wind and snow.

Callie didn't think about it too hard. It was another sign this plan of hers was going to work. She parked the improbable bike in a rack next to the library, counting on the fact that it was old enough no one would try to steal it.

The blast of heat as she walked inside propelled Callie, already warm from her ride, out of her coat and scarf. She hung them on the coatrack by the door, then turned to see Esme the librarian beaming at her. Today she had bright purple lipstick to match even brighter purple cat-eye glasses.

"You're back! Calliope, right? Are you here to sign up for a library card?"

Callie pulled the book Esme had given her the last time from her backpack. "Um, yeah," she said. "I loved this one. Thanks for loaning it to me."

"That's what we're here for!" Esme took the book and gave it a fond stroke. "*Goodbye Stranger*. It's one of my favorites. Have you read any of her others?" She pulled the paperwork for a library card out and set it on the counter between them.

"I've read *When You Reach Me*." Esme made a hand-to-forehead swooning motion and Callie grinned. "I was also wondering . . . do you happen to have a book club?"

"A book club?"

"Like . . . a regular gathering for kids. Or anyone, I guess. To talk about books."

"I'm afraid not, love. Or rather, we have a book group, but it's all old biddies my gran's age. I don't think it would quite be your speed. Although you're welcome to come! Their next book is"—she consulted a sticky note on her computer screen—"*Flower Arranging for Dummies*."

"Oh." Callie's heart sank. Somehow she didn't think flower arranging with a bunch of senior citizens would fulfill her parents' requirements. "Thanks anyway."

Maybe she could convince Esme to start a book club for younger people. If not, Callie was going to be stuck doing a sport or taking an acting class.

She tried to get up the nerve to suggest it as she filled out the paperwork for her library card. She didn't know the castle's address, but she wrote down Spence Castle and figured that would be enough. How many castles could there be around South Kingsferry?

Finally, she asked.

"I don't think I'd get much interest in a kids' book club because the schools have their own," Esme said. "But the librarian at the high school is fantastic. Have you started there yet?"

"I'm not going there. But thanks."

"Oh." Esme's eyes widened but she didn't ask any questions.

Callie hurried away from the desk, not wanting Esme to see the tears welling up. Who cried over a book club? But it was so much more than that. Was she willing to chase a ball around a field or dance in front of an audience, if those were the only ways to get out of going to South Kingsferry High School?

She tried to ignore the thumping of her heart as she headed upstairs, where she distracted herself by picking out some new books to read. Then she headed down to the nonfiction section to get some books for her history project, realizing as she did that the Brits might tell the story of the American Revolution somewhat differently than she'd always heard it.

When there was nothing more to do in the library, Callie approached the checkout desk. If she couldn't come up with a brainstorm between here and the castle, she was going to be pulling on a uniform before she knew it.

Esme tapped on Callie's selections. "You've got excellent taste. But ooh, I haven't read this one." She held up a book Callie had chosen purely for the cover, because judging a book by its cover was sometimes a very good idea. "You'll have to tell me how it is. We can have our own little book club of two."

Callie mustered a smile, but as much as she'd like to talk books with Esme—and she definitely would—she knew it wouldn't count for her parents' homeschooling condition. She needed peers. Preferably introverted ones who would also enjoy sitting quietly and reading. Maybe she could join the high school book club without enrolling in the actual school? It seemed unlikely, but Callie was desperate. She carefully stacked her finds inside her backpack for the ride home. "Thanks," she said. "I'll be back soon."

"I'm counting on it," Esme said. And then, before Callie reached the door, "Here, Calliope, do you have any interest in twitching?"

* * *

"What on earth is twitching?" Mom asked, still in the stables and covered head to toe with sawdust.

"It's bird-watching, I guess. There's a group that meets at the library twice a week." Callie crossed her fingers hard.

"A group of . . . kids? Your peers?" Her mom narrowed her eyes at Callie. "Bird-watching?"

It had sounded weird to Callie, too. But Esme made it sound fun. She'd done it as a kid, and she'd certainly turned into someone Callie would like to be. "I guess it's a whole thing here. They have competitions and everything."

Mom didn't look convinced. She handed Callie a stack of the cut boards and lifted a stack of her own. "Help me carry these to the staircase and tell me more about it."

There wasn't much to tell, but Callie emphasized the social part of it as much as possible. She'd told her mother everything she knew long before they reached the castle's front doors.

"Twice a week?" Mom asked.

"Plus extra outings and competitions and stuff," Callie said. She didn't know a raven from a crow, but bird-watching sounded like a non-sporty, non-performance activity she'd happily do if it meant she could avoid the high school. The fact that it met at the library was a bonus.

"All right," Mom said, readjusting the stack of boards in her arms. "I guess that sounds like it'll fit the criteria."

"Yes!" Callie had never imagined she'd be so excited about the prospect of staring through binoculars at birds. But it wasn't about the birds. She'd won! No high school. No schlubby weirdo. Learning on her own and wandering the castle grounds like some sort of Mary Lennox–Anne Shirley–Lucy Pevensie mash-up! It was still a reinvention—just different than she'd planned.

Callie hauled the boards inside and plopped them at the foot of the stairs. Then she ran back out to where she'd left the old bike and her pack when she'd gone to find her mom. "Thank you!"

"Your father has to agree!" Mom called, but Callie wasn't worried. If Mom agreed, Dad would be a cinch.

She dropped her pack on the steps to the castle and started wheeling the bike toward the stables. No reason to take it all the way back to the cottage, but she couldn't leave it in the middle of the driveway, either. The stables seemed the most reasonable place for it.

She was exhausted from the ride—it had been easy to get the hang of riding again, but also more tiring than she remembered—so she was moving along slowly when a sharp voice called out to her.

"What are you doing with my bike?"

Callie turned and to her complete astonishment, a girl around her own age stood glaring at her, hands on hips, expression fierce.

"What do you mean, your bike?"

The girl marched over and yanked the bike away from Callie. "I mean what I said. This is my bike. And you . . . you stole it!"

"Hang on a second," Callie said, heart starting to pound at the unfounded accusations. She had been in this situation before. "It was on the grounds, by the cottage. I'm Callie Feldmeth. We . . . my family, we own the castle. And the grounds, so . . ."

"So you own everything that happens to be on the grounds? If the milkman drives up your lane to deliver a liter of milk, do you own the lorry because it's on the grounds?"

Callie wasn't even sure what a lorry was, but the answer was clear. "Of course not, but—"

"My grandpop and I are going to be on the grounds for a while, looks like, and I'll thank you not to be stealing my things every time I turn around!"

Before Callie could offer any further explanations, the girl swung herself onto the bike and rode away in the direction of the pond.

The night it all turned ugly, Callie had never felt prettier.

She was a peacock, sparkly silver-green and blue. If she looked down just right, she could see the shimmer on her own cheeks, but mostly she was looking up, arms raised,

JOY McCULLOUGH

dancing to the music streaming from Imogen's speakers.

She thought they were having fun, doing makeovers. They'd done it before. She didn't think Lyla was serious when she said they should sneak down to the high school bonfire at the beach. Kate said they'd need to look older if the boys were going to talk to them.

Callie didn't really want high school boys to talk to her.

But she gave in to the whirlwind of makeup and perfume and borrowed clothes. They were pretty, shiny things, and for a moment there, Callie thought herself a magpie, collecting the glittering attention of her friends.

But she wasn't a magpie, not really. She wasn't a peacock, either. She didn't know then that the female of the species is called a peahen, drab and brown and not meant to be noticed.

8 September 1939
Inverness

Though there will be far graver losses in this blasted war, my peacock-blue jumper is the casualty I'm mourning just now. (I immediately want to scratch that out, because I'd trade every single thing I own or ever will for my brother Charlie to avoid the front. It's only that this notebook is a place for my feelings or whatnot, and Father always does say I'm prone to the dramatic. If this isn't the time for dramatics, I don't know when is.)

Mrs Miller said it was washing day. And honestly, it was about time, since they'd only allowed us to bring one small bag each, half of which was taken up by a gas mask. I don't even know why we had to bring those. The whole point of sending us away is that no one would bother to bomb the Highlands.

I wasn't sure where I was meant to leave my things, since our room doesn't have a dumbwaiter like at home, which is where Helen sets my basket of clothes to be washed. I thought I was being helpful by gathering my things and setting them in the hall outside our door.

But then June asked why they were there for everyone to trip on and I said to be collected for washing and Magda said who are you expecting to collect them and I didn't have an answer. Then she laughed like I'd told the funniest joke and asked if I expected the other girls to do my washing and I said of course not and finally they left (with their own dirty things), and all the way down the hall Magda pretended to be me, complaining in a loud, snooty lady-of-the-manor voice how tiresome it was to be without her butler and her nanny and her cook and her personal lady's maid.

I do not have a personal lady's maid.

I waited until I saw them all out of doors and playing at something besides tormenting me. Then I gathered my things and took them downstairs to the kitchen. I might have asked Mrs Miller for help, but I was ashamed, so I did my best to wash my own things in the sink and hung them to dry on the patio.

Now my favourite jumper is four sizes too small.

CHAPTER SEVEN

"I'm sorry we haven't kept you up to date on every single decision we've made about the renovation," Callie's mom said with a huff as she hauled more wood from a rented truck in the courtyard outside the stables. She needed a helping hand, but Callie wasn't feeling especially helpful right then.

"I don't see how you could forget to mention there's a girl living on the castle grounds! A girl my age!"

"Shouldn't this be a good thing? Honestly, Callie, the lengths you'll go to avoid having friends—"

"That's not what I'm—"

Callie stopped. Maybe that was what she was doing. But

even if she did want to make friends, it certainly wouldn't be with that girl, who refused to hear her out. Callie hadn't stolen the bike! Or at least, she hadn't meant to!

Mom reached the stables and set down her load. "I'm sorry you got off to a rough start, but there'll be plenty of time to make things right. We've hired the girl's grand-father as our chief landscaper. They'll be living in the cot-tage for a while."

"Your cottage?"

Mom laughed. "Well, it's all ours now, isn't it?"

"But the one you and Dad lived in before?"

"Yes, across the pond. It's the perfect space for two people. Mr. MacDonald's granddaughter lives with him, so you'll have to figure out how to deal with her presence. There's a thousand acres. Somehow I think you'll be able to avoid each other."

Except they couldn't. Every time Callie turned around, the girl was there. When Callie played hide-and-seek with Jax—now with clear rules about avoiding the pond—the girl scowled from where she perched on a crumbling stone wall. While Callie ferried things back and forth from the castle to Mom's workshop in the stables, the girl zoomed past on the contentious bike and practically ran Callie over.

It put an awful dent in Callie's plans to become an independent soul who wandered the moors, unaware of the outside world.

Even sitting in her beloved window seat in a bedroom out of a fairy tale, Callie caught a glimpse of the girl, strawberry-blond braid swinging, skipping rocks across the pond. From a distance, unaware she was being watched, the girl looked a lot less scary. In fact, she almost looked lonely.

But that was silly. The girl obviously didn't want friends. And just because she was alone didn't mean she was lonely. Callie knew that better than anyone.

The girl's grandfather was the opposite of scary. Callie met Mr. MacDonald one morning when she came downstairs to find him in the kitchen, landscaping plans spread all over the table. Jax was shooting baskets into the Nerf hoop he'd attached to the far wall, but other than that, there was no one else in the room.

"Mornin', lass," the older gentleman said. "Excellent timing. I'm trying to decide between Dunwich roses or Stanwell Perpetuals for this border here." He pushed a flower catalog across the table and pointed out two different types of roses. "What do you reckon?"

Callie blinked at him. "Um."

"Callie doesn't know," Jax said. "Unless you want to plant books, she can't help you."

The man chuckled. "Aye, wouldn't that be a thing, though? Planting books? What do you reckon would grow if you planted a book?"

Callie had no idea what to say. Esme would probably have a great response.

She was saved from having to answer, though, when her dad came in. "Sorry about that," he said. "I find the reception's better in the great hall. The wholesaler was delighted to hear how many rosebushes we'll need."

And then they were off, droning on about landscaping details while Callie got her cereal and settled onto the couch to eat it. The man's Scottish accent was so strong she didn't understand everything he said, but his voice was soothing, a lullaby.

When he and her dad were done discussing the landscaping details, the old gardener rolled up the plans on the table and winked at Callie.

"What'll it be, then: Dunwich or Stanwells?"

"Dunwich, I guess," Callie said.

"Excellent choice! Well done! I think you're about my granddaughter Cressida's age. You should swing by the cottage and meet her sometime."

We've met, Callie didn't say. *I stole her bike and she yelled at me and we'll never be friends.*

"Okay," she said.

Callie wasn't a lot more hopeful about making friends at her first meeting of the South Kingsferry Youth Twitching Club. But at least everyone there would be a birder, which probably leveled the playing field in terms of social status.

She shut out Imogen's voice in her head, telling her how dumb the idea of a birding club was. How could you form a club around watching birds? What was she, eighty? And why the heck did they call it "twitching"? It sounded like a dance move, one the chaperones tried to keep kids from doing.

Esme's bright, happy face the moment Callie walked in the library doors was an excellent way to shut Imogen up.

"Hello, love!" she called out. "Already need some new books?" Her lips were orange today, and something glittery shimmered on her cheeks.

Callie slid her returns across the counter. "I finished these. I'll get a couple more today, but I'm here for the . . . birding group?"

Esme grinned, like she knew Callie couldn't bring herself to say twitching. "Downstairs in the meeting room."

"Thanks, Esme."

"Here, Callie," Esme said, right as Callie reached the stairs going down. "Mr. Hunt can be a bit of a git. But no one else in the whole region knows more about birds."

"Okay, thanks."

The tables in the nonfiction area downstairs had a number of people working at them, lots in the South Kingsferry High uniforms. Callie gulped and kept her head down as she beelined across to the meeting room.

The door was closed, but there were still three minutes

left before the meeting was scheduled to start. Callie eased the door open and found every face staring at her. They were all boys, sitting in folding chairs formed into a circle. Most wore the high school's uniform, their ties loosened or removed. The leader was a tall, balding man around Callie's dad's age.

"Can I help you?" he said.

"Um," Callie's eyes flew to the clock. "Sorry, I think I'm early, I'm here for—"

"We have the room for the next hour," the man interrupted. "Knitting group's at four."

Knitting? Nothing against knitting, but had he really said that? Callie's eyes took in the birds projected on the screen behind the man.

"No, I—I think I'm in the right place."

"Calliope?"

Her eyes flew to the friendly voice—Rajesh from the school tour, who knew her as Calliope. Who she'd run out on when she panicked for no good reason.

"Hullo!" He stood and pulled another chair into the circle. "Mr. Hunt's always starting early. This is Calliope," he told the rest of the group. "She's American."

Mr. Hunt frowned. "Right, then," he finally said. "As I was saying. This week there was a spotting of a red-footed falcon in the Pentland Hills Regional Park. Their numbers are in sharp decline, due to habitat loss, so if you can get out there to add this very interesting bird of prey to your life lists, I highly recommend it.

"Moving on: either you lads are not recording your sightings into the spreadsheet, or you're not keeping up like you ought to be. We will take the youth club record for number of individual sightings in the year, but only if you each do your part."

Callie looked around the circle. One particularly haughty-looking boy (though honestly the ties made them all look way snobbier than was likely true) rolled his eyes, but several boys stared at their hands, and a couple mumbled, "Sorry, Mr. Hunt."

"All right," Mr. Hunt said. "If that's all the business we've got to take care of, I thought we'd use the rest of the hour to walk down to the dock and see if we can't finally add an ivory gull to your lists." He turned on Callie. "What sort of binos do you have?"

"Sorry, what?"

"Binoculars," Rajesh supplied.

"Oh, I don't have any."

Mr. Hunt gave a long-suffering sigh. "How do you propose to see any birds then?"

"With my . . . eyes?" Callie hadn't meant it to come out snarky. It simply hadn't occurred to her that there might be a better way to see them.

"She can use mine," Raj offered. "We'll work together."

Mr. Hunt huffed and led the way out of the meeting room. Callie didn't like disappointing adults, but Mr. Hunt didn't exactly inspire her to win him over. Esme gave a hesitant little wave to Callie and a questioning eyebrow quirk as the group trudged past the reception desk. Callie shrugged. She'd never imagined she'd be happy to get out of a library, but the brisk air and the distance from Mr. Hunt's judgment were welcome.

"Don't mind him," Rajesh said. "Nobody has binos their first meeting, unless their folks are hard-core twitchers or something. Which my mum is. I'm sure we have extras you could use."

"I'm sorry about before," Callie blurted as they turned off the high street onto a narrow alley that led down toward the water. The cobblestones were more uneven here and Callie stumbled. Raj grabbed her elbow, and one of the boys behind them snickered.

"What? The meeting? You weren't late—"

"No, at the school. The way I ran off."

Rajesh looked genuinely confused. "I mean, I don't blame you. I'd've run out of there too, if I could. Anything to avoid the next Taco Tuesday."

Mr. Hunt halted the group to point out a kestrel on a nearby rooftop. A couple of boys pulled out phones, and Callie expected Mr. Hunt to chastise them, but he nodded approvingly and kept moving.

"They're listing the kind of bird," Rajesh said. "It's their first time spotting it." He pulled a tiny notebook from his jacket pocket and handed it over for Callie to look. "Most people use an app, but my mum makes me do it old-school."

Callie flipped through the pages. It was divided up into columns, listing dates and times and places, the names of bird species, space for notes about behavior. Raj's book was almost full.

"Wow. How long have you been doing this?"

"Since I was a newborn and Mum took me out, strapped on her back." Rajesh took the notebook back. "I mean, my list isn't that old. My handwriting was a lot worse when I was a baby."

They had reached the shore. The two massive bridges loomed on each side of the village, crossing the glassy water and coming together on the opposite shore, a perfect example for a young artist learning about perspective. The dock jutting out into the water made an almost U shape, with boats docked inside the U and enough room to maneuver out of the U and into the inlet. To one side of the U, more boats were docked, and to the other, a couple of elderly men stood with fishing rods. On either side of the dock, water lapped gently against a tiny pebbled beach.

"All right, gentlemen," Mr. Hunt called. "And lady.

Let's cut the chitchat, unless your goal is to scare away every bird in the vicinity!"

The seagulls on the dock didn't look the slightest bit scared.

"An ivory gull has more of a pigeon shape than your traditional gull," Mr. Hunt went on quietly, like a golf announcer on TV, "and its body is pure white. The yellow bill is red on the tip, and its legs and feet are black."

Apparently finished with his instructions, Mr. Hunt found a spot along a stone wall next to the dock and sat, attentive, his binoculars perched on his knees.

"So we just . . . wait? And hope the bird will come?"

Rajesh grinned. "It's more exciting than it sounds. I mean, maybe not if you're used to extreme sports. Or competitive spelling bees."

Callie snorted.

"Oh, you laugh, but spelling bees are dead serious. I should know. My sister was UK champion last year."

"Wow!"

"Yeah, she got all the competitive genes in our family. I prefer birding. Less opportunity for complete humiliation." He held up the birding journal. "So you keep a list of all the species you've seen. Sometimes you go out with something in mind, like Mr. Hunt wants us to find an ivory gull today. There's kind of a thrill when you find what you were looking for and add it to your list."

Callie was not convinced, but she didn't want to be rude to the one person who was talking to her. And it was better than playing soccer. They walked a ways out on the dock and plopped down next to a heavy rusted chain. A rumbling sound called Callie's attention to the red bridge, and she realized a train was crossing it. Looking in another direction, she could see the curving shore and the row of shops on the high street, this time from behind.

And if she twisted around behind her, she saw the sailboats moored in the center of the U shape. When she paid attention, there were birds in all directions.

"So pick a bird, any bird," Rajesh said.

"Any bird? I thought we were looking for a specific—"

Rajesh waved his hand. "Any bird."

Callie scanned her options—the water, the bridge, the shore, the dock. Possibilities everywhere. A smallish bird with black wings, a brown body, and a spot of white around its tail was perched on one of the dock pilings. "That one."

"Ding ding ding!" Rajesh said. "You win a storm petrel! Not a rare bird, exactly, but unusual to see one here this early in the year. They don't look like much, but they're super tough."

A storm petrel.

"So that's your first bird," Rajesh said. "For your list. Do you have a phone?"

Callie shook her head.

"Then you do it old-school, like me. When you get home, start a list with the date and place and the species you see today, starting with that storm petrel."

"Oi, Frodo," one of the boys shouted, and the storm petrel startled, then flapped away indignantly. "Got yourself a Yankee girlfriend?"

The other boys guffawed and more birds took flight. Mr. Hunt walked over, glaring at Callie. "Enough distractions," he said. "If you're not serious about birding, I suggest you don't come back."

9 September 1939

Inverness

Rosie found me sobbing into my ruined jumper
and offered to give me a lesson in washing, but
getting a lesson from a seven-year-old was more
mortification than I could bear.

She's sweet in the rare moments it's only
the two of us. But if Magda's around, Magda
is queen, and none of the others will ever be
friends with me.

That's fine. I'm not here to be best chums
with any of them. The only thing we have in
common is parents who thought we'd be safer
with a stranger than our own families.

My best chums are Anne and Diana, and they're
stuck back in Kingsferry, as though it doesn't
matter if bombs drop on them. When I told
Mother they're my best chums, she laughed and
told me dogs can't be chums, which shows you
how much she knows.

Mrs Miller doesn't have a dog. Only chickens
and some sheep. I thought the sheep might be a
comfort to me, since they're furry at least, but
their eyes are completely empty and they offer
nothing back for my affections.

Still, I've begun to venture outside. Not to play with the others, but simply to wander, as it's better than staying cooped up in a room filled with cots, and anyway Mrs Miller caught on to my "headaches" pretty quickly.

Today I saw a bird I'm almost certain was a storm petrel. Father pointed out a storm petrel the last time we were sailing. This one had the same fluttering flight, almost like a bat. But the odd thing is storm petrels spend almost their entire lives out at sea. They only come to land during the breeding season, and now is definitely not that.

Father scorns superstition, but he showed me the storm petrel because it's supposedly a bad omen for mariners. They say a storm petrel foretells bad sailing conditions. But the truth, Father said, is storm petrels need rough winds to support them while they fly. If the weather is calm, they float on the surface of the water.

So they don't bring the bad weather at all. They only use it to their advantage. In other words: they're misunderstood.

CHAPTER EIGHT

Callie hurried to the ivy-covered church, fighting to steady her breathing and her voice before she reached her dad. The red that had no doubt risen in her cheeks could at least be explained by the wind. Dad stood proudly beside a car somehow smaller than the rental they'd gotten at the airport.

"What do you think?" he said, beaming. "I got a great deal!" He'd gone to pick up the used car while Callie was in her meeting, and as he slipped inside, he already looked more comfortable in the right-hand-side driver's seat.

"Why are the cars so small here?" Callie grumbled, folding herself into the passenger seat.

But she regretted asking, because Dad rambled on about how wasteful Americans were, how they needed everything to be so big, how they guzzled so much petrol— he actually said "petrol," not "gas"—and basically acted like he was fully Scottish himself. His lengthy monologue was at least a distraction from having to tell him about Mr. Hunt, so that was something.

He only asked how her meeting had gone when they turned onto the long, twisty road leading to the castle. Their home.

"Not great."

Dad, being Dad, didn't ask anything more.

If it weren't for the stupid socializing requirement, Callie would drop the birding club in a second. Mr. Hunt had been awful. Rajesh was really nice, but not nice enough to make up for the rest of the boys, who looked at her like she was some kind of mutant. She should have known she'd be the opposite of Venetia Charles, waltzing into her San Diego elementary school with her sophisticated accent and stylish clothes.

"Run over to the stables and tell Mom I'm back with the car, will you?" Dad parked in front of the castle. "I have to make a quick call to a plumber we've got to hire."

Callie scowled at the first bird she saw when she climbed out of the car. It could go on her list, if she knew what it was. Not that she cared about her list. Stupid *twitching*.

When she heard voices as she approached the stables, she assumed Mom was listening to one of her podcasts while she worked. Callie's favorite to eavesdrop on was one with two grown men discussing each Baby-Sitters Club book. But instead of a lively discussion about the best babysitter, Callie walked in and nearly collided with Mr. MacDonald. And his granddaughter.

"Ah, it's my rose-selection assistant!" the gardener cried. "Hello, lass."

"Hey, hon," Mom said. "How was bird-watching?"

Mr. MacDonald's bushy eyebrows jumped up. "Are you a twitcher, then? My Cressida here has quite the eye for the avian creatures as well."

"Sid," Cressida mumbled, staring down at her black high-top Chucks with rainbow laces.

"Aye, yes." The gardener looked deeply chagrined. "I forget sometimes, but she prefers to go by Sid."

"I'll see you back at the cottage, Pops," Sid said, then made a break for it.

Mr. MacDonald frowned. "Apologies. I dunno what's gotten into her lately. Well, anyhoo, thanks for taking these things off our hands."

That was when Callie noticed the jumble of boxes stacked inside the doors to the stables.

"Oi, Callie," he said on his way out. "Cressida told me you're in need of a bike. I noticed one at the secondhand. Shall I grab it next time I've got my truck in town?"

"That would be lovely," Callie's mom said when she didn't answer.

"Thank you, Mr. MacDonald," Callie finally said, distracted.

"Oh, call me Ben, lass." He tipped his hat and headed out.

Had Sid told her grandfather that Callie *needed* a bike or that she'd *stolen* a bike?

"What is up with you?" Mom asked when Mr. MacDonald had shuffled out of sight. "That was very nice of him."

"I know. I'm sorry." Callie's eyes landed on a cool old-fashioned trunk that hadn't been there in the morning. "What is all this stuff?"

"Oh, just junk that was stored in the cottage. Ben and his granddaughter need a bit more space to move their things in, so I told him they could move this stuff here to the stables."

"What's inside?"

"I honestly have no idea. Probably dishes and moth-eaten blankets. You can go through it all later, if you want, but right now I really need you to go put some water on for pasta, pretty please?"

* * *

Putting water on for pasta turned into making the entire dinner, but Callie didn't mind. Cooking was familiar, even in a very unfamiliar kitchen. Tomato sauce and ground beef were always going to turn into the same delicious comfort food. The only colander she could find to drain the pasta was massive, which would come in handy if she ever needed to make pasta for the entire village.

Not that she was exactly making village friends right and left. She pictured Mr. Hunt as she forcefully sliced cucumbers and carrots for a salad. "I'll give you knitting classes," she muttered.

"What?" Jax piped up.

"Nothing. Set the table."

By the time her parents showed up, the room smelled amazing and they showered her with thanks for being so responsible. When her family asked over dinner about the birding meeting, Callie told them about the storm petrel and then changed the subject to Jax's first soccer game.

If she quit birding after one meeting, they'd make her go to the high school. But she kept hearing Mr. Hunt's voice in her head: *Enough distractions.*

She hadn't done anything except exist.

CHAPTER NINE

The castle grounds in the evening were like something out of an eerie movie, all mists over the rolling hills and dusky light and straggling rabbits making for their burrows before the danger of night fell completely.

Loose gravel crunched beneath Callie's feet as she made her way out toward the stables, camping lantern in hand. A birdcall startled her and she tripped, but as soon as she righted herself, she scanned the nearby trees. An owl, maybe? During the day there was so much bird chatter on the grounds, she wouldn't know where to look. Evening was different, though. Hopefully the rabbits would all make it home.

The doors to the stables were heavy and Callie had to set down the lantern and use both hands to haul them open. Inside, the power tools and Mom's partially finished projects cast looming shadows in the light from the lantern. Callie turned on the work lights, which made things only slightly less creepy.

Mr. MacDonald—Ben—had stacked the boxes from the cottage on the opposite side of the stables from where Mom had set up shop, so her work lights didn't quite reach. Callie hauled a few cardboard boxes closer to the light.

A cloud of dust rose as she pried the lid open on the first one. Coughing, she pushed aside yellowed newspaper to find—as Mom had predicted—old dishes. They were cool, but not the sort of treasure Callie was after. She didn't know exactly what that was, but she'd know it when she found it.

Everything had changed the day Lady Whittington-Spence died and left the Spence estate to Callie's family. But also, nothing had changed. Arriving in Scotland and living in a castle hadn't made any kind of difference in who Callie was. The birding meeting didn't make her into a budding scientist or naturalist. But she refused to believe she was stuck with the Callie she'd always been.

When Mary Lennox arrived at Misselthwaite Manor, she discovered the secret garden. When Lucy Pevensie was evacuated to the Professor's country home, she discovered the wardrobe. There had to be something for Callie to discover that would change everything.

Jax had wanted to come with her to the stables when he heard about the possible treasure, but Callie had been quick to point out the hazards of Jax and power tools and improper supervision. For once, her parents hadn't dumped him on her.

The next box held holiday decorations—ornaments and nutcrackers and a Nativity set. Callie grabbed a marker from her mom's toolbox, labeled the Christmas stash, and set it to the side. Those would come in handy later in the year. Though it was hard to imagine Callie's family would be here at Christmas. It still felt temporary, like a vacation, or a dream.

The next few boxes were less exciting—linens and encyclopedias and boring legal papers. Callie labeled each box and set them to the side. She was about to grab a few more from Ben's stack when she spotted the old-fashioned steamer trunk she had seen before. Like something the Pevensie siblings would have packed when they were sent off to the country to escape the war in London.

Now *that* looked promising.

A few latches on the side of the trunk unhooked easily, but front and center was a sturdy lock. And Callie had no key.

Picking a lock did not turn out to be as easy as it seemed in movies. Callie tried. But when she left a deep scratch in the wood around the lock, she backed off. The trunk itself was part of the treasure. It was probably an antique, and she didn't want to damage it.

She couldn't get it open right now. But she had the best feeling about this trunk. She wasn't going to leave it out here with the tools and random boxes, either. With a great deal of pushing and shoving and hauling and some language she wouldn't have used in front of Jax, Callie got the trunk onto a dusty dolly and rolled it to the front doors of the castle.

"Dad!" she called. "I need help!"

The trunk was the perfect addition to Callie's bedroom, especially after she found some rags and scrubbed the years of dust and grime off the wood, the metal panels, the leather handles.

"I don't understand what you want with a trunk you can't open," Mom said as she stopped in Callie's doorway on her way to bed, shivering in her ratty UCSD sweatshirt.

"I'll get it open," Callie said. Dad's muffled voice drifted over from the room next door, where he was reading aloud to Jax. "Anyway, the mystery is part of what's cool."

Mom smiled. "Like something from a book."

"Exactly."

Callie didn't dream of the contents of the mysterious trunk. That would have been too easy. Instead she tossed and turned as seagulls screamed their way across clear blue San Diego skies. They never stopped, the gulls. They were endless, and they were everywhere, bold and brazen.

Now they were weaving in and out of the gleaming white sailboats tucked into their slips in a marina somewhere between San Diego and Scotland. It could have been either. But it had to be San Diego, because the pristine ships were girls from Callie's school, girls she'd grown up with, indistinguishable from one another, pretty at a glance, even glamorous, but pull any one of them out onto dry dock, and you'd see the underside of its hull, all crusted with salt, black with the scum of algae and mold and barnacles that had latched on, thinking they'd found a place to belong, unaware they'd be scraped off at the earliest opportunity.

Then the screaming got louder, piercing, and Callie was sitting up in bed and the screaming was still slicing through the night, except it wasn't a screaming so much as a clattering and a deafening kerfuffle, and Callie was just awake enough to realize it was coming from her fireplace.

She ventured out of bed, welcomed by an ice-cold floor, and tiptoed over to the fireplace. The night outside was pitch-black. If she'd been more awake, she might not have done what she did next, but she'd just been in a marina with terrible gulls and barnacles and mold, and something in her fairy-tale bedroom was in distress, and Callie moved aside the grate covering the fireplace.

When the creature swooped past her face and into her room, Callie wasn't entirely certain whether she was still in the dream. It wasn't the glaring bright marina anymore, and this wasn't a seagull, but dreams were funny that way. Only when Jax threw her bedroom door open and shouted, "What the heck?!" did Callie know this was really happening.

"Is that a bat?" he yelled.

Callie was wide-awake now, but the black winged thing was moving too frantically for her to be sure what it was.

"I don't know!" She rushed to the heavy leaded windows and tried to pry them open to give the creature a way to escape, but the windows were stuck fast. "Get Mom or Dad," she told Jax.

For the briefest moment, the creature landed on one of the posts of Callie's bed, and she saw the same beady eyes, the same sharp, powerful beak she'd seen through her window that first day.

"A raven," she breathed.

This raven had been stuck in her soot-covered chimney, and as it took off from its perch once more, soot rained down on Callie's beautiful bedspread and pillows.

"There is not a vampire in Callie's room," she heard Dad say right before he and Jax stepped inside.

"It's a raven," she told them calmly. "And it's afraid, so everyone needs to stay calm. Dad, can you help me get the window open?"

Eventually Mom had to run out to the stables for a crowbar, since the windows apparently hadn't been opened since Lady Whittington-Spence had been a child. Finally the frigid air rushed into the room and the raven flew toward the familiar, the darkness.

Long after the bird was free, the window shut, and her bed linens replaced, Callie sat, imagining the raven stuck in the pitch-black of the chimney, the unforgiving stone on every side, no room to stretch its wings. In Callie's bedroom at least it could fly, but the harsh light and strange surroundings and frantic humans might have been even worse than the chimney.

Part of Callie thought the crazed, desperate raven was a sign that she shouldn't have anything more to do with birds. But she stayed awake the rest of the night, wanting to know everything about that raven.

CHAPTER TEN

In the morning light, sooty evidence of the raven's ordeal coated every surface in Callie's room. Black and gray tufts of feathers floated down as she moved. In the middle of the desk sat a single gleaming feather the length of Callie's forearm.

She took it over to the window seat and held it up to the light. It was the blackest black, but somehow it was also purple and blue and green, depending how she moved it. She set it back on the desk and went to the fireplace, getting down on her hands and knees so she could stick her head inside and look up. It was shockingly black inside—coal soot, Mom had said the night before, was almost impossible to clean.

At least the raven was already black. But would all the sticky stuff clinging to its wings impair its flight? Had the soot gotten in its eyes?

After much scrubbing, all traces of the raven were cleaned away from the bedroom, except for the magnificent feather on Callie's desk. Still, she couldn't stop thinking about the bird. She imagined Mr. Hunt's voice, chiding her for opening the grate and letting the bird inside. But if she hadn't done that, wouldn't it have stayed stuck in the chimney?

Did ravens have families that would miss them if they were stuck somewhere? Or would the raven's flock reject him now because of all the human smells on him? People said not to touch a baby bird because its mother wouldn't let it back in the nest if it smelled like humans. She hadn't touched the raven, but the bird had been all over Callie's bedroom.

There was no way she could ask Mr. Hunt any of this, even if she did return to the bird-watching group. Ben had said that Cressida—Sid—knew a lot about birds. But she was no more a possibility for help than Mr. Hunt.

Maybe Esme would know, or at least she could help Callie find out.

"Any luck with the trunk?" Dad asked at breakfast.

Callie shoved the scrambled eggs across her plate.

"No. You haven't found a drawer full of keys around here, by any chance?"

He laughed. "Sorry, no. Though I do remember once when we lived here, I was helping Lady Whittington-Spence move some furniture and I found a neat old-fashioned key underneath a dresser. She had no idea what it was for and told me to throw it away. But I kept it."

Callie perked up. It was a long shot that this was the key she needed, but it was better than nothing. "What did you do with it?'

"Oh gosh, hon. It was so long ago. I don't remember."

Out in the stables, Mom didn't remember either. "Honestly, Cal, there are so many cool things to explore around here. I wouldn't give that old trunk much more thought. Can you hand me my safety goggles?"

But Mom didn't understand. She had a purpose and a place she belonged. Callie was not giving up on the trunk.

Jax's first football game was played on a soggy field behind the primary school. On the other side of the field, neat little rows of houses sheltered together—similar to the San Diego neighborhoods where the houses all looked the same, but a totally different style, more compact. Like the Dursleys' neighborhood, but not a movie set. It felt foolish now to imagine that number 4 Privet Drive had sprung from J. K. Rowling's wild imagination when really it was faithful to actual UK neighborhoods.

"Fits right in, doesn't he?" Dad said.

Callie located Jax on the field, where he blended in with his team full of boys and girls in bright blue jerseys and white shorts. Like he'd known them all his life.

("White shorts?" Mom had groaned when they got the uniform.)

Jax wasn't the best player on the team, having been more focused on baseball and basketball back home, but he was a natural athlete and a born leader, and before the first quarter was over, he was the one his teammates turned to when they celebrated any goal or well-placed defensive move.

He was also absolutely, completely plastered in mud.

"That your brother?" said a voice right behind Callie as they stood in the drizzle on the sidelines.

Out of his school uniform, Rajesh looked even younger. He swam in a sweatshirt with a complicated crest printed with the words HEART OF MIDLOTHIAN SOCCER CLUB.

"Oh, hi," Callie said. "Do you have a sibling on the team?"

"Nah, I just fancy standing around in the rain and watching terrible young players trip all over themselves." Rajesh burst out laughing at the look on Callie's face. "I'm joking you. The keeper on the red team, that's my sister."

"Oh, hello," Mom said, returning from retrieving a garish plaid umbrella from the car. "We met you at the school, didn't we?"

"Right you are. I'm Raj." He stuck his hand out to shake Mom's. "Calliope's little brother is a solid footballer."

Mom's eyebrow twitched at the use of Callie's full name, but thankfully she didn't say anything. "Thank you! Jax is our little athlete. Do you play?"

Raj shuddered. "I did for a bit. But then all my class-mates grew and I didn't." He pointed out his sister as she smartly deflected a goal. "Nah, Damini's the competitor in our family."

"Is she the spelling bee champion too?" Callie asked.

"Aye. I'm expecting she'll go on to be an Olympic medalist who cures cancer and discovers a way to make brussels sprouts delicious."

Jax was more of a goofball social butterfly than a standout overachiever, but either way he always grabbed the spotlight too. Even though Callie didn't really want to be in the spotlight, sometimes she wished there was a way to get a little of the glow, at least.

"Who's this?" Callie's dad asked, turning away from the conversation he'd been having with the parent on his other side. "I'm Callie's dad, Pete."

"This is Raj," Mom said a little too brightly. Like it was such a miracle Callie had met someone her age. "We met him at the high school."

"And we're in the twitching club together," Raj added. Callie winced. "We are, right?" he whispered as her parents turned their attention to Jax heading for Raj's sister at the goal.

Jax managed to get the ball past the keeper, and Callie's parents erupted in cheers. Callie cheered along with them, and Raj yelled to his sister, "You'll get 'em next time, Damini!"

"You're coming back, right?" Raj asked when the game had moved on. "To the twitching club?"

"I don't know." Callie shoved her hands in her hoodie pocket. "Mr. Hunt's kind of . . ."

"A numpty?"

"A what?"

"A numpty. A tube. An absolute roaster?"

Callie burst out laughing. "You are making these words up."

"I am not. I believe you would say 'a jerk,' but we Scots prefer more colorful insults."

"Yeah?"

"Oh yeah. For example, next time one of those bampots from the twitching club says something rude to you, here's what you say back: Awa' an' bile yer heid."

"What?"

"You heard me. Awa' an bile yer heid!"

"That's not English."

"It's Scottish." He said it again, but more slowly.

"Are you saying"—Callie was laughing so hard she could barely get the words out—"'away and boil your head'?"

"That's it now! You're sounding Scottish as anything."

Raj entertained Callie through the rest of the game—or match, as he called it—with increasingly hilarious Scottish insults. By the time the game ended—Jax's team lost, but Jax scored their only goal—Callie's sides ached from laughing.

Raj's mom made her way over to meet them once she was done handing out snacks to the players. "Hello," she said. "I'm Bina."

She looked like an older version of her son, but with longer hair. Not a lot taller, though. As Callie listened to the parents chatting, she thought Raj's mom had a different accent than most of what she'd been hearing in Scotland.

"Your mom's accent," she said to Raj. "Is it Scottish?"

"Nah," he said, "my parents are Londoners. But we moved here when I was a baby so Da could open his company's Edinburgh office. Damini and I sound mostly Scottish, though, since we've always lived here."

Callie loved the Scottish accent. She wished she could put it on and have it fit like her favorite jeans. But she knew it was like the stiff school uniform, not meant for her. Jax might take on the Scottish brogue—he was little enough it wouldn't feel so odd. But on Callie it would be forced, fake. She was stuck with the plainest of American accents.

"I'm so glad you made a friend," Mom said in the car on the way home. "Any chance you might like to give the high school another thought?"

There was no chance at all. Callie could see Raj at the birding club. And it wasn't only that she didn't want to go to the high school. It was also that she wanted to keep doing the things she was doing. She'd found a rhythm with her days that she kind of loved. She got up and wrote in her journal, first thing. After breakfast, she did her science and math programs online. Then she read, and after lunch she worked on her *Hamilton* project. Her parents couldn't deny she was holding up her end of the bargain.

She hadn't quite reached full Mary Lennox–Anne Shirley–Lucy Pevensie, but she was getting there. It was close. If she could only open the trunk.

15 September 1939

Inverness

Question: Is it possible to feel both utterly
ashamed and totally victorious at the same time?

Answer: Yes, yes it is.

Today we were trapped inside because of
torrential downpours. I considered sneaking
out, but I suspect I wouldn't have seen any
interesting birds, which have become my main
pastime in my wanderings, because they would all
be taking shelter as well.

Mrs Miller made me join the others in the
drawing room for board games. She sat there,
watching us, so I had no choice but to play.
We settled on Anagrams. At one point I played
the word "Bach," and Magda said I'd misspelled
"back," and honestly I was very nice about it, but
to defend myself I informed her Johann Sebastian
Bach was a German composer, which of course led
to comments about how high-and-mighty I am.

Mrs Miller could have said something, but she
only left to check on our tea.

Then Magda tried to play the word
"lavoratory." I challenged her, for that is not
a word. She insisted it was a place where

~~ 113 ~~

scientists do experiments. And I said, "Maybe if they're experiments done on toilets?"

I couldn't help blurting that out! Because a lavatory is a washroom! And a laboratory is where scientists work! And the other girls EXPLODED with laughter, and I'd never seen Magda so angry. She ran off and hid in the room for the rest of the night, and I felt horrid, I did, but also I felt relieved that finally I wasn't the outsider.

CHAPTER ELEVEN

Callie rode her very own bike to the next birding meeting.

She had been sitting in her window the evening before, reading Esme's latest recommendation, when she saw Sid ride up to the front doors on a different bike from the one Callie had borrowed. (Stolen? The whole thing was fuzzy.) It wasn't brand-new, but it was nicer than Sid's, red with chrome handlebars, and with a basket in front that would be perfect for bringing books to and from the library.

At first Callie thought Sid was riding up to the castle with a question or a message for one of Callie's parents. But she parked the bike and walked away from the castle without speaking to anyone. This was the bike Ben had picked up for Callie in town. At least, she was almost sure. But she refused to touch it until her mom texted him to double-check. She didn't want to risk riding another unauthorized bicycle.

Since the bike had been verified as 100 percent hers, Callie set off the next morning along the mile-long driveway to the main road leading into town. It was a smoother ride than Sid's bike had been, but still bumpy, and Callie almost wiped out again when her front wheel hit a sizable rock halfway down the lane. But she righted herself and only swerved into the tall bushes a little bit.

Esme was busy with another patron when Callie arrived at the library, so she waved and dropped her returns on the cart on her way downstairs. She had arrived a full ten minutes early, now that she knew how Mr. Hunt operated. She didn't need to be his favorite birder, but the twitching club would be a lot more bearable if he didn't hate her.

"Hello, Mr. Hunt," she said as she took a seat. Only a few boys had arrived, and Raj wasn't among them.

Mr. Hunt looked up from his notes. "Young lady, I understand you are residing in Spence Castle at the moment?"

"Um, yes?" The other boys looked up with interest at this bit of news. "Not only the moment," she added. "It belongs to my family now."

Mr. Hunt narrowed his eyes and swallowed a response with some difficulty. Instead he said, "The castle grounds would be an excellent location for a birding excursion, if your parents would allow that."

"Oh," Callie said, pleased to be not only not annoying, but also potentially helpful. "I'm sure they'd say yes."

He nodded curtly. "Ask them, please. Update me next time."

A few more boys had filtered in, but still no sign of Raj.

"We'll start when I return," Mr. Hunt said, slipping out of the room.

"How does your family suddenly own the castle?" one of the boys said. "Are you related to the Spence family?"

"Aren't you American?" asked another.

"She could be American and still related," someone else interjected. "Like, Meghan Markle, duh."

"She didn't marry a prince, Jacob," the first boy said.

"I'm right here," Callie said. All the boys turned to look at her.

"Well then, answer the question," Jacob said.

"My parents were close to Lady Whittington-Spence," she said. "They lived in the cottage before I was born, when they were students at the university. She left the estate to them in her will."

The boys looked at Callie for another second, then turned back to one another.

"My mum says she had no other family."

"No kids, maybe, but you'd think there'd be cousins or something."

"Shouldn't it be, like, a national monument?"

Mr. Hunt returned before the boys could further dissect Callie's right to live in the home her family now owned.

"All right, lads. Today we'll be doing a warm-up version of our Big Day competition later in the spring. Working in pairs, you'll have one hour to spot as many different species as you can. Your boundaries are the clock tower to the pharmacy, and the shore on up to the Tesco. We'll meet back here to compare notes."

The boys all started to move, pulling binoculars and phones from their bags.

"Remember," Mr. Hunt said, "you may not count a species on your list unless you have spotted a male."

The boys nodded and began to move for the door.

"Wait, why?"

Mr. Hunt glared over at Callie. This wasn't going to be a point in her favor, but she couldn't contain herself. "Young lady, in this country we ask questions with proper decorum."

Color rose in Callie's cheeks, but she wasn't going to let this go. Why on earth should a female bird not count as a sighting? It was bad enough that she was the only girl in the group. She'd done some investigating on birding websites, and it seemed like most of the birding record holders were men too. Why should male birds and birders get all the glory?

She thrust her arm into the air. Mr. Hunt returned to his instructions for the day's excursion, but Callie kept her hand in the full Hermione position.

"Mr. Hunt," one of the boys said. "I think Callie has a question."

Mr. Hunt didn't chastise the boy for his interruption, but turned instead on Callie.

"What is it?"

"I know I'm new to this," Callie said, "but I don't see why a female bird shouldn't count as a sighting."

"Be that as it may," Mr. Hunt said, "those are the rules."

"It's just"—Callie ignored Mr. Hunt's huff—"I've been researching outside of these meetings too, and I know the female birds often have duller colors or less showy feathers."

"Plumage," Mr. Hunt corrected.

"Right. Which seems to me it would make them trickier to spot." Mr. Hunt waited for a beat, then opened his mouth to continue. Callie went on. "So it would take a more skillful birder to spot them."

One of the boys let out a childish "Oooooh," as though Callie had said something totally offensive. The others snickered. If Raj had been here, he would have understood what she was saying.

"In this club," Mr. Hunt said, his ears turning bright red, "we follow the instructions of the leader with decades of experience, and not the abject beginner who has attended one and a half meetings. In order for birds to count on this or any other list, you must have spotted a male of the species."

He said it like the case was closed. But it wasn't.

How could he say half the birds out there didn't count? Just because they were female? Callie knew she was right that female birds would be trickier to count, but that shouldn't even matter. Even if male and female birds looked exactly the same, she had a feeling that Mr. Hunt would still say they could only count male birds.

"That's completely unfair!" Callie was on her feet now. She'd never exploded like this at a teacher or any adult, really, but this was not a flood that could be held back. This was the injustice of doing the right thing and losing all your friends in the process. This was being judged for how you looked, or how you were different, or how you weren't what some arbitrary decider said you ought to be. "It's a stupid, sexist rule! If you were a good enough birder, you could see the females, too!"

Mr. Hunt marched to the meeting room door and opened it. "That will be quite enough, young lady. You may spot all the female birds you'd like on your own time, for you will no longer be participating in this club."

The boys were silent.

Callie grabbed her bag and held her chin up as she stalked out of the room, but tears streamed down her face before she reached the top of the stairs. Esme looked up in alarm as Callie rushed past the checkout desk. She heard the librarian calling after her with concern, but she bolted out the doors and to the bike rack. Esme came all the way outside, but Callie was on her bike before she had to make any explanations.

In her room, Callie bashed the trunk's lock with a hammer she'd snatched from the stables. She left horrible scratches on the metal of the lock and dented the wood all around it, and still she couldn't get in.

"What's wrong?" Jax asked in a small voice from the doorway. He'd opened without knocking, which was strictly against the rules, but there was too much else for Callie to be upset about right now.

"Nothing," she said, realizing how completely ridiculous that must sound as her eyes were puffy from crying and she was wielding a hammer like a madwoman.

Jax crept over and sat down next to her. He leaned his head on her shoulder. "I thought you liked it here."

"I do," Callie sniffled. At least, she had.

"Better than San Diego, right?"

She nodded.

"Your friends there were jerks."

Callie looked at her little brother in surprise. He'd always been so wrapped up in his sports and friends and happy-go-lucky life that she hadn't thought he'd known anything about her San Diego friends. "Absolute roasters," she said.

"What?"

"It's Scottish for jerks," she explained. "I'm trying to get this trunk open."

Jax nodded. "Mom says it's an 'exercise in futility.' From the sound of it, you were getting exercise, at least."

Callie handed over the hammer. "Want to try? It's kind of fun."

Jax didn't need to be asked twice.

CHAPTER TWELVE

Jax ducked out of Callie's reach as she tried to ruffle his hair on his way out the door the next morning. The first time she'd seen him in his school uniform, she'd said he looked cute, and he'd objected mightily, so now she made a point of treating him like an adorable toddler whenever she saw him in uniform.

"Have a good day at school, my little munchkin!" she called as he climbed into the car with Mom, scowling.

Callie's dad chuckled behind her. "You two," he said. "All right, I'm going to be in the keep this morning, assessing the damage. Where are you going to be?"

"The keep? Can I come?"

The keep was the one part of the castle Callie hadn't gotten to explore. Whenever she asked her parents, they said she couldn't go alone. Lady Whittington-Spence's lawyers had been very clear that the keep in particular was in serious disrepair. In olden days, the tall tower between the two larger sections of the castle had been a lookout for invaders, and the strongest and most secure part of the castle, where the nobility could hide if invaders got through the first lines of defense.

Callie's parents were renovating the castle so tourists could come and enjoy it, with historically accurate rooms for people who wanted to stay overnight. The keep was going to be the big moneymaker, with several rooms— including a banquet room for medieval feasts. But there was a lot of work to be done first.

"Not yet, Callie-kins," Dad said. "I need to get a better handle on the situation before I let you or Jax in there."

"But I could—"

He held up his hand to stop her. "Nope. You've got work to do, don't you?"

Callie sighed. It was another injustice. She was way lighter than her dad. If anyone shouldn't be allowed in the keep, it was probably him. "Fine. I'm going to wander around and listen to my audiobook."

He grinned. "Sorry to twist your arm into such a dreary activity."

"I can at least walk you over there," she offered.

"I would welcome the company."

Outside, the orchestra of morning birdsong was in full swing. The sky was a shocking blue against fluffy white clouds, and the emerald expanse of grass twinkled with dew. The whole thing looked like it had been drawn with the brightest crayons in a kindergartner's box.

"I still can't get over the trees here," Dad said.

They were massive. The sort of trees sure to contain hidden doors leading to entire worlds of elves or gnomes. Magical, gnarled trunks and branches had twined around one another over decades, centuries. Every shade of green distinct, but also part of a whole.

As they headed toward the keep, a raven swooped overhead, fierce and powerful. Callie hoped it was the chimney raven, recovered from his trauma. Or her trauma. Callie hoped it was a female raven, if only to spite Mr. Hunt.

Dad followed her gaze. "Did you know there's someone at the Tower of London whose entire job is to care for the ravens there? He's called the Ravenmaster. Legend has it that if there aren't six ravens living in the tower at all times, the fortress will crumble."

"Are they like pets?" Callie asked. "In cages?" How else would they ensure that the ravens stayed? Unless their wings were clipped, like Lyla's parakeets.

"I'm not sure," Dad said. "You should ask your birding leader about them."

Callie's gut twisted. She hadn't told her parents about being kicked out of the birding club. She hadn't meant to lie to them. She simply didn't know how to tell them. She'd never been kicked out of anything. And she wasn't sorry about how she'd acted. Plus, she didn't need to hang out with a bunch of bampot boys twice a week to prove something to her parents.

"Okay," she said. They stopped at the entrance to the keep. "I really want to go up there, Dad."

He smiled and kissed Callie on the top of the head. "I know. And you will. Have a good walk."

Callie sighed and pulled her iPod out of her pocket. She ran a longing hand across the rough stone of the keep and turned away from it. The entire castle grounds stretched out before her—a thousand acres. She didn't really have a sense of how big that actually was. All she knew was there was so much of the estate she hadn't explored at all.

She had been avoiding the cottage since Ben and his granddaughter had moved in, but every evening from her bedroom window, she saw a flock of very small birds diving into one specific tree on the far side of the pond. She'd never seen anything like it, a whole flurry of birds, more than could possibly fit in one tree. But they must, because after they disappeared into the tree, there was stillness. Every night.

Callie would walk all the way around the pond and see if she could spot these little birds up close. It was the perfect time, since Sid would be in school. Not that Callie didn't have every right to wander the castle grounds.

She had always thought of a pond as a tiny body of water, like the one with koi outside her dentist's office in San Diego. This pond was more like a lake, big enough that a walk all the way around took twenty minutes. The whole time her family had prepared for Scotland, Callie's parents kept referring to their move "across the pond," meaning the whole Atlantic Ocean.

So maybe there were no limits to the size of a pond.

Partway around, Callie spotted Ben trimming an overgrown hedge. He noticed her and waved his clippers at her. When Callie finally reached the opposite side of the pond, she scanned the nearby trees, trying to figure out which one was home to the flock of little birds she saw every evening.

But while the particular tree was obvious from her bedroom window across the pond, Callie stood at the water's edge facing dozens of trees. It could be any of them. She turned back to face the castle, counting up and over from the main doors to pinpoint her window seat. It didn't really help.

From the outside, she didn't see birds in any of the trees, though she heard plenty of birdsong. Determined, she drew closer to the nearest tree and looked straight up. Would she see a nest? Or nests? It seemed like hundreds of little birds swooped into the tree every night. Surely they would leave some sort of evidence.

If there were nests, the tangle of branches was too thick for Callie to spot them. She moved on to the next tree.

"What are you looking for?" a voice asked. From up in the tree.

Callie stumbled back, tripped on a root, and landed on her rear end. Whoever had spoken didn't laugh, which was something. Callie peered up into the branches. She could just make out a pair of shoes. Black high-top Chucks with rainbow laces.

"Cressida?"

"It's Sid."

Ben's granddaughter didn't move any farther down from her perch, and Callie could still see only her feet. "What are you doing up there?"

Her answer floated down: "Plotting global domination."

Callie paused. "You don't go to school?"

"The world is my textbook," Sid said.

She was homeschooled. At least that wahs what it sounded like. Maybe they had more in common than Callie had thought. Her neck was starting to hurt from craning it up to peer into the branches. "Do you mind if I come up?"

Sid shifted where she sat, and a twig fell down to knock

Callie on the nose. "I mean, you do own the whole castle grounds, so . . ."

It was a dig, a subtle reminder of the bike incident. Callie could have turned and retreated back to her lavender room, to her books and her fireplace and her rolltop desk. She almost did. But she'd stood up to Mr. Hunt. If she thought about it too hard, she started to panic. But if she squinted at it sideways, it made her feel sort of powerful. And she suspected Sid wasn't anywhere near as scary as Mr. Hunt.

Callie considered the tree. She didn't know the last time she'd climbed one. San Diego mostly had palm trees, which weren't ideal for climbing, unless you were a monkey. She managed to grab onto the lowest branch but wasn't sure how to get her leg over it. She felt Sid's eyes on her, but the expert tree climber offered no additional instructions.

Finally, through a combination of bracing a foot against the trunk and flailing her free limbs wildly, Callie made it onto the first branch. Getting any higher would be even trickier. But now she could at least see Sid's face.

"I hope you know I didn't mean to steal your bike," Callie said. "But I'm still sorry."

Sid sat in stony silence, eyes focused somewhere behind Callie's head. After an awkward moment, she got a funny expression on her face, then blurted, "What were you looking for? In the tree?"

"Oh." Callie clung to the trunk as she lifted herself to stand on her branch. "I'm looking for these birds I see from my window in the evening." If she grabbed onto a branch above her head, she'd be steady enough to step up to the next branch. Once she'd done that, she wedged herself into a space between the trunk and a sturdy branch only a few feet down from Sid's perch. "There's like a million of these birds. They're small. I think. But I'm looking from far away, so . . ."

Sid waited. Then she said, "Small? Is that all you can describe? Aren't you in the twitching club?"

"Not anymore," Callie said. Then she looked up with wide eyes. "But don't tell my parents?"

Sid shrugged. "Don't tell my pops I was up in a tree. Do they swoop around in cool formations?"

"Yes! And then they all sort of dive into the tree together."

"Starlings." Sid declared the bird species as confidently as Jax would name his favorite baseball team. "They look plain from a distance, but if you see them up close, they've got really cool colors. There can be thousands of them in one tree, sometimes."

"Oh. Thanks." Callie peered into the branches above them.

"Not now, though. They take off in the mornings. That's neat to watch too, if you're up early enough."

It was hard to believe this tree was big enough to hold thousands of birds. But then, it was managing to hold Sid and Callie at the same time, and they were two different solar systems. "You really don't go to school?"

"Pops and I move around too much. And I'd rather be alone."

Again with the stony stare. Callie could take a hint. "Oh. Okay. Sorry to bother you. I'll go."

Sid didn't object, so Callie looked down for the first footrest of her descent. She reached it easily, but then she couldn't figure out where to step next.

"You're going?" Sid asked.

Callie peered up at her. Of course she was going. Sid had basically told her to go. "I'm trying."

Sid leaned way out over her branch to assess Callie's situation. "Move your left foot a little farther over and there's a branch," she said.

Callie looked up at Sid. "Thanks." And that was when she saw the chain around Sid's neck, and hanging from it, an antique key.

18 September 1939

Inverness

Magda has had her revenge.

    She didn't act the night of the Anagrams
humiliation. I was prepared for her then. But she
waited until I let my guard down. And then she
poured a pitcher of freezing water over me while
I was sleeping.

    The way I screamed made the entire household
come running, thinking bombs were being dropped
or worse. Mrs Miller was furious with ME, for
"overreacting," she said. Overreacting?! Magda
is the one who overreacted to a failed Anagrams
word!

    Then Mrs Miller punished us BOTH by sending
us to clean out the chicken coop, which is
maybe the most disgusting thing I've ever done
in my entire life. At least I wasn't terrified
of the chickens, like Magda. For a girl who
acts like I'm the haughty princess, she couldn't
stop moaning about getting near a few feathered
friends.

    I find chickens fascinating. When a chicken
gets its head cut off, it can still run the length
of a football pitch before it drops dead. And

there are more of them in the world than humans.
So they're survivors.

I could do without shovelling their poo, though.

CHAPTER THIRTEEN

Callie could not stop thinking about the key. The chance that Sid was wearing the exact key she needed to open her trunk was absurd. But everything was absurd these days. She was living in a castle! She was climbing trees and picking fights with authority figures, and she'd even tried haggis, a sort of sausage made from sheep's entrails. If she didn't think too hard about how it was all stuffed inside the sheep's stomach lining, it wasn't too disgusting. But that fact was pretty hard to ignore.

The conversation in the tree had been a step, but Sid was obviously touchy about her belongings. It could be disastrous to imply that the key she wore as a necklace actually belonged to the trunk, which was a part of the castle, which belonged to Callie's family. It would definitely erase any progress they had made toward being friendly-ish.

Jax had no such difficulty making friends. After only a couple of weeks of school, he'd already brought friends around the castle grounds and gone off to play at their houses. His mates, he called them. He was definitely picking up a touch of the accent.

Callie assumed Jax was off at a mate's house when she had a peaceful afternoon working on her history project and he never once appeared to pester her. But then her mom asked her to track Jax down for dinner.

"Where is he?"

"Oh, the grounds somewhere." Mom waved her hands vaguely.

That could mean anywhere! It wasn't like stepping out into the apartment courtyard back home.

"He went looking for Ben," Dad added. Which didn't really narrow things down much. But it gave Callie somewhere to start. And maybe even a reason to talk to Sid again.

When she made it to the cottage on the other side of the pond, Sid didn't answer the door. Callie's heart sank, only partly because she wouldn't have a chance to try again with Sid, but also because she still hadn't seen inside the place where her parents lived all those years ago. Then a nearby splash sent her heart careening from disappointment to panic.

She tore around the side of the cottage. Why was she obsessing over a key and a stupid old trunk when she should have been paying attention to Jax?

She stopped short at the sound of Jax's laugh and then another laugh—but it wasn't Ben's. She crept forward. Standing at the edge of the pond, Sid was bent double, cracking up as Jax heaved a massive rock into the water. It made the same loud splash Callie had heard moments earlier.

"A stone, I said," Sid gasped. "It has to be a stone! A small one. Look." She crouched down and picked out a few stones from the shore. She handed one to Jax. "Flat and smooth, if you can find them."

Gone was her prickly sarcasm; Sid spoke to Callie's brother like a totally different person. A soft, open person.

"Good," she said. "Now keep it level, like a tiny Frisbee." She showed him how to skip the stone across the surface, her own stone plopping merrily along five or six times before sinking into the dark gray water.

Jax tried again with the right-size stone and let out a grunt of frustration when it skipped only once.

"None of that," Sid said, bumping him gently with her shoulder. "That was good, it was. Most folk don't get it on the first try."

"Natural stone skipper, is he?" Ben appeared from around the other side of the cottage, so Callie was still hidden from the view of all three of them.

"He's not bad," Sid admitted.

"I'll be better than Cressida as soon as I practice," Jax boasted, and Sid didn't correct him about her name.

"Oho!" Ben laughed. "That'll take quite a lot of practice, laddie." He swung his arm around his granddaughter's shoulder and gave her a squeeze.

"You okay, Pops?" Sid asked, her brow furrowed.

He muttered something Callie couldn't hear. Then, louder, he said, "How about some hot cocoa?"

"Yes!" Jax said.

"Sorry." Callie stepped forward, and they all turned in surprise. "Thank you for the offer, but Jax has to come home for dinner."

"Callie! I can skip stones! Wanna see?"

"I saw," Callie said. "You keep practicing and you'll be better than Sid in no time." She snuck a glance at Sid, who grinned. "Thank you for hanging out with Jax."

"Why are you thanking her?" Jax said. "I'm amazing."

Ben chuckled. "Lassie, will you tell your father I couldn't finish getting the roses in today like we'd planned? I'll get them in tomorrow."

"I will, Ben," Callie assured him. She turned to follow after Jax, who was already running toward the castle. But first she shot a cautious smile at Sid. "Seriously, thanks."

Sid had already turned her attention to her grandfather, who she was urging toward the cottage door. "Come on, Pops, let's get you off your feet. I'll heat up some soup."

The next day Callie was sitting in the kitchen finishing her math when the heavy front door knocker sounded. She figured it was an electrician or plumber or one of the many other workers who'd been arriving over the last several weeks. Instead she found Sid on the doorstep.

"Oh, hi."

"Hi." Sid fidgeted with the drawstring on her hoodie as blustery wind whipped her hair around her face. "Is your dad or mom around?"

"My mom's out in the stables, I think. But um . . . Dad?"

No answer came back through the cavernous space. "I think he's in the billiards room. I can show you?"

Sid nodded and stepped inside.

"The wind is wild here," Callie said. Then immediately regretted it. Was weather really all she had to talk about?

Sid said nothing, which made sense. What was there to say about wind?

Callie led her down the hall to the billiards room with its springy floor, which had been used for dancing before it was mostly covered up with the massive pool table. Sure enough, Dad had his tools spread out on the hearth and was working to repair the damaged masonry of the room's fireplace.

"Dad? Sid's here."

Callie's dad set down his trowel and sat back, his forehead covered in a thin sheen of sweat, despite the frigid temperature in the room.

"Hello, Sid. What are you girls up to?"

Callie flushed at the suggestion that she and Sid might have plans. Like they were friends. Not that she didn't want to be. But she couldn't tell whether or not Sid wanted to be. It was all so confusing. How did Jax make friendship look so easy?

"Actually, Mr. Feldmeth," Sid said with strange formality, "I came to tell you my grandfather isn't going to be able to get the rosebushes in today like he said he would. He's not feeling well."

Dad stood and ran a hand through his messy hair. "I'm sorry to hear that. Is there anything we can do?"

"Oh, no. He's just a little run-down. He said he could manage, but I made him rest."

"He's lucky to have you looking out for him." Dad wiped chalky dust from his hands. "Would you like to join us for lunch, Sid? We could send some food back for Ben as well."

"Oh no, I couldn't." Sid pulled her hoodie tighter.

"It's up to you. We'd love to have you. I promise it's warmer in the kitchen."

By the time they'd reached the kitchen, Dad had convinced Sid to stay. It wasn't for his cooking, which consisted of warmed-up enchiladas from the night before. But Sid talked easily with Callie's dad, like she had with Jax. She told him about the various parts of Scotland she and Ben had lived in. She asked him questions about California.

"You guys don't ever settle and live in one place?" Dad asked Sid.

"Pops goes where the work is. I go where Pops is."

Callie wanted to ask where Sid's parents were, but she thought better of it. Whatever magic Dad and Jax worked on Sid, Callie couldn't seem to access it.

Sid went cool and stony only once, when Mom came in to grab some lunch for herself.

"What are you girls up to?" Mom asked, exactly like Dad had.

Callie started to protest, but Sid said, "Just eating lunch, for now."

Something in the way she said it—*for now*—made it sound like it was possible they *could* be hanging out. That maybe they would be later.

"I'm sorry to hear Ben's under the weather," Mom said.

That was when Sid did her thing. Quiet, no response, her fork paused halfway to her mouth.

Mom frowned for half a second, then shook it off. "All

right. Well, I'm heading back out to the stables. Trying to get those cabinet doors cut before I have to go pick up Jax."

"I should get back to work too," Dad said. "Callie-kins, you done with your math? Can you clean up the dishes?"

Callie winced at the babyish nickname, but if Sid thought there was anything wrong with it, she didn't show it. "Yeah, of course."

Callie stood to clear the dishes, and her dad left the room. Instead of rushing to leave, Sid stood and brought her dish over to the sink. "I'll help," she said. "Wash or dry?"

Callie blinked at her. "Whatever you want."

Sid washed while Callie dried and put away the dishes.

Maybe Sid actually was lonely. Or maybe she didn't want to go back to the cottage and disturb her grandfather while he was resting. The weight of that, being responsible for an aging relative when Sid wasn't even a teenager yet—it was unimaginable. It was a weight greater than the wheelbarrow full of bricks Callie's dad had hauled into the billiards room to repair the fireplace.

Maybe it felt nice to share that weight for as long as it took to share leftovers with someone, whether she liked the person or not.

Or maybe, possibly, Sid wanted to be Callie's friend.

"Can I ask you a question?" Callie finally said.

Sid handed her the last dish and wiped her hands on a towel. "I guess?"

"What's that key you wear around your neck?"

Sid's hands flew to the key, like she thought Callie might yank it off. But she shrugged, casual. "It's nothing. I found it."

"Where?" Callie asked. "I'm not . . . I don't want it or anything. I'm just curious."

Sid considered her for a moment. "Here, in the cottage. Pops and I had to move all the stuff to make room for our own things. Not that I'm complaining. This is the nicest place we've stayed in forever."

"All the stuff you moved into the stables?" Which had included the trunk.

"Yeah, the boxes and stuff."

Callie paused. She could be cautious and play it cool, waiting for some other moment to present itself, some time when she was more sure of Sid's reaction. If that time ever came. But it probably wouldn't. Sid was here now. She'd chosen to stay, not only to eat, but to help clean up. "Will you come with me up to my room? I want to try your key in this trunk I have up there."

Sid took a step backward, like she thought Callie was bonkers. "I really doubt it's the key you're looking for."

"Can we at least try?" Callie said. "You'll get to see more of the castle."

Callie bit her lip as she waited for Sid's response, focusing on the tiny stab of pain rather than the anxiety of what Sid might say.

"Okay," Sid finally said.

Flooded with relief, Callie led the way to the grand staircase.

"Wow," Sid said when she saw the state of the renovations—half the stairs ripped out and replaced with bare wood; a bunch of the wall paneling removed; giant, probably priceless paintings stacked together against the wall on the floor.

"I know," Callie said. At the moment, it looked even worse than when they'd first moved in, with various renovation projects started but not completed. "My parents have big plans. For now, at least we're not freezing to death at night anymore."

Callie was halfway up the stairs when she realized Sid was still at the bottom. "My room's up here," she said.

Sid was staring at the wood-paneled wall. She probably didn't want to go to Callie's room; it had been stupid to invite her up. Just because she'd answered a couple of questions about birds and helped wash some dishes didn't make them besties.

Callie knew the trunk wasn't going to contain glamorous clothes that would instantly transform her, or a genie in a bottle who could grant her wishes. But she really wanted to find out what was inside—whatever it was.

"If you don't want to come up, could I at least borrow the key?"

No response.

Imogen had regularly deployed the silent treatment, but Callie usually had at least some sort of idea why.

She came back down the stairs. "Sid?"

Finally Sid looked at her. "Are we going up to this trunk, or what?" She headed up the stairs.

Callie followed, exasperated. This girl made no sense.

At the top of the stairs, Sid waited. "Which one?" she asked, motioning to the long hallway of doors.

"Mine's down here," Callie said. As soon as she opened the bedroom door, she felt self-conscious. Anyone with a name like Cressida who preferred to be called Sid wasn't a lavender flowers kind of girl. "I go by Callie," she blurted as Sid took in the room.

This time Sid looked at her immediately. "I know. That's what your family calls you."

"I've been introducing myself as Calliope. I thought . . . new country, new name. I don't know, it's dumb."

"It's not dumb. Names are important."

Names clearly mattered to Sid, the way she corrected her grandfather when he called her Cressida.

"Have you always wanted to be called Sid? Is Cressida too . . . flowery?"

Sid traced a finger over the purple buds on the wall-paper. "I like flowers. Cressida's just . . . someone else. From a different time. Do you want me to call you Calliope?"

Callie had never been asked what she wanted to be called. Everyone had always assumed. When new teach-ers at the beginning of a school year would struggle with her name, one of the kids who'd known her forever would holler, "She goes by Callie!" But now . . . now she had a choice.

"I don't know."

Sid shrugged. "Tell me when you decide." She pulled the chain with the key from around her neck. "Moment of truth?"

"Right!" Callie took the key and knelt in front of the trunk. She half expected Sid to walk out of the room or stare out the window, but she sank onto the threadbare rug next to Callie.

The key went into the lock almost too perfectly. Both girls gasped.

"I knew it," Callie breathed. When she turned the key, she heard a click. The latch on one side of the lock popped open, but the other one didn't.

"Maybe you turn it again?" Sid suggested.

Callie tried, but nothing happened.

Sid leaned forward to look more closely. "The latch is kind of bashed in. Maybe that's why it won't release."

Callie had a sinking feeling, thinking of how much time she and Jax had spent assaulting the lock. And all that time, Sid had been holding the key that could have opened it easy as anything.

"Have you ever thought," Sid asked, "that opening an ancient trunk might not be the best idea? Kinda sounds like the start of a horror movie to me."

"Can't be more of a horror movie than the crazed raven swooping around my room the other night." Sid's eyes widened and Callie told her the story, possibly making the raven bigger and more terrifying than it had really been. "Anyway, my mom says it's probably old blankets."

"Then why do you want to get in so badly?"

Callie couldn't possibly explain it to Sid when she hadn't been able to figure it out for herself. She knew it would sound dumb if she tried to put into words the idea that this trunk might be her secret garden or magical wardrobe. She knew it wouldn't literally transport her. And anyway, she'd already been transported to the new, magical place. But something was still missing, and it might be inside this trunk.

"I mean . . . why are you wearing a random key around your neck?"

Sid thought for a minute. "I guess it just . . . seemed mysterious."

"Exactly." Callie pulled the key out and tried inserting it again.

Sid scooted around to the back of the trunk. "What if we took off the hinges back here?"

Removing hinges would require different tools than the hammer Callie had been using to bash the lock. Luckily, she knew where to find plenty of tools. And even more luckily: Mom wasn't in the stables.

"She probably went to the keep to check on Dad," Callie said. She grabbed the electric drill and the case of drill bits from the workbench.

"Wouldn't a screwdriver work?" Sid asked.

"This'll be easier. But you can grab one, just in case." She nodded to the toolbox, and once Sid had picked out a screwdriver, they headed back to the castle. Callie was glad to slip out of the stables unseen by her mother, because strictly speaking, Mom probably wouldn't be thrilled by her using power tools unsupervised. But it was only an electric drill.

"Why does your brother go to school, if you don't?" Sid asked.

"Because he likes people," Callie said.

Sid snorted. "Weird."

Back in Callie's room, they pulled the trunk out so they could both reach the back, where heavy-duty hinges were attached with metal screws. If they could unscrew the hinges, they'd be able to open the trunk from this side and forget the lock altogether. Callie took the drill out of its case and made sure the correct drill bit was inserted.

"You know how to use that thing?" Sid scooted away as Callie tested the drill in the air.

"Yeah. Do you want me to show you?"

"No, thanks."

Callie shrugged. It seemed odd that Sid roamed free and hung from the highest tree branches but was anxious about a power tool. But Callie was happy to do it herself. The drill was one of the first tools her mom had taught her to use. She put the drill in reverse and lined it up with the first screw.

It was a lot more difficult than using a drill on fresh screws. These were old and worn down, and the drill kept jolting off the screw. Sid startled every time. But Callie was so close! There was no way she was stopping now! Finally the first hinge was free of its screws.

"Come on," Callie said, offering Sid the drill. "Taking off the hinges was your idea. You should help. You line up the pointy part and then pull this trigger-like part. You sort of press in while the screw is coming out, which seems like the opposite of what you'd want to do, but it helps keep it steady."

Sid looked doubtful. But she took the drill. "Only one," she said. She followed Callie's instructions exactly, and the first screw of four on the hinge came off. She shoved the drill back at Callie. "You do the rest. It's your big mystery."

The last three screws came out with a bit of struggle, but soon enough Sid was helping to pry the hinge off. The girls each took a side and lifted the lid. It wouldn't flip all the way open because the lock was still half-fastened on the other side, but they were able to force it wide enough to see in. Sid grabbed a log of wood from the stack by the fireplace and wedged it in to hold the lid up.

The first thing Callie saw when she peered inside was a scratchy wool blanket. Mom had been right after all. But Callie didn't even mind. This was an impossibly old blanket. Who had it belonged to? Where had it traveled? She reached in and pulled it out.

Under the blanket was a jumble of things. Sid pulled out a stack of books—a dictionary and a thesaurus and some history textbooks. Callie pulled out a pile of sweaters and scarves. She sneezed at the dust.

Sid held up a pea-green sweater. "It looks exactly your size," she said.

Callie wrinkled her nose at the hideous garment. Not everything vintage was cool. But some things were. She wrapped a plaid scarf around her neck and tossed a stylish felt hat to Sid.

Finally, from the bottom of the trunk, Callie pulled a shoebox tied with twine. Everything they'd found already had been exciting in its own way, even the scratchy blanket. But this box—too heavy to actually contain shoes—held the promise of a wardrobe with snow falling at the back.

She struggled with the knots, and Sid pulled a Swiss Army knife from her pocket. She looked at Callie with the question in her eyes—was it all right to cut?

Callie pushed the box toward Sid, and she sliced through the twine. Callie lifted the lid off the box and gasped.

19 September 1939

Inverness

Shovelling chicken poo has inspired me.

At first I was angered by how extreme Mrs Miller's punishment was. An afternoon of hard labour for screaming when doused with freezing water? That was a punishment that did not fit the crime!

That was like when I was six and Charlie twelve, and I asked him to cut my braids off, so he did. Then Mother sent him away to study at Gordonstoun so he'd "learn discipline" and not be a bad influence on me, and after that I only ever saw him on holidays.

Soon he'll be getting fired upon by German soldiers, and I may never see him again.

Mother seems determined to send her children away, but I am determined to get back. To be with my dears Anne and Diana. To see Father on the rare occasion he comes home from London. And perhaps, if I am honest, in the hopes that Charlie will be sent home from the front and I'll be there to welcome him.

I'm mortified to admit that hope, since he'd only be sent home if he were too maimed to continue in battle, but maimed is not dead, and I would care for Charlie for the rest of his life if it meant having him back at Spence where he belongs.

So all this is to say I've realised Mrs Miller's outlandish punishment may have been a gift in disguise. If my hostess is prone to doling out excessive punishments, it would likely not be that difficult to get myself sent away completely.

CHAPTER FOURTEEN

Nestled carefully in yellowed newspaper sat a pair of binoculars. They looked a million years old, with the black worn off where fingers had held on, exposing the metal below. Callie stared. Part of her wanted to grab them, but she didn't want to break them, or break the spell around them.

"Are you going to try them?" Sid asked.

Then again, the binoculars had been sitting in a box inside a trunk for who knew how long. Binoculars were meant to be used, and clearly these had been used a lot. Callie touched the cool metal and felt the roughness where the black coating had worn off. She picked the binoculars up and examined them. Engraved on the black above the eyepieces, it said KERSHAW OF LEEDS, and in smaller type below that, 6 X 30.

She handed them to Sid, who held them up to her eyes. Then she moved over to the window seat and pointed her gaze out the window. After adjusting them for a moment, she said, "Whoa."

Callie followed her. The view was already magnificent without binoculars. Sid handed the binoculars to Callie and showed her how to adjust the focus. Callie aimed them at the tree across the pond, where the swarms of starlings danced at night. It took a while to get the focus perfect, but once she did, *whoa* was right. Even at this distance, she could see the definition of the leaves. She could see a bird—not a starling, something bigger, with a crest on its head.

"Wow."

"Hey, there's more!"

Sid was back at the shoebox, lifting the newspaper nest out. She brought the box to the window seat and held it out to Callie. Callie traded her the binoculars and reached into the box for a bundle of yellowed booklets tied together with twine. The top cover said BIRD NOTES AND NEWS, VOLUME XXI. Beneath it there was a London address, and the rest of the cover was filled up with a pen-and-ink drawing of a fearsome-looking bird, something like an eagle.

"What is that?" Callie asked, holding it up to Sid.

She shrugged. "I dunno. What? I'm not a nature encyclopedia."

The pieces started to click together in Callie's brain. She raced over to the rolltop desk and pulled out the leather journal. The list of birds.

"These must have been Lady Philippa's," Callie said.

"Who's that?" Sid asked.

"The lady of the castle. The lady who left it to my parents. I found this journal in the desk—it's got a list of birds in it."

Sid flipped it open to the inscription on the inside cover. "How old would she have been in 1939?"

"Um." Callie knew Lady Whittington-Spence had been very old when she died, but not exactly how old. She started to do the math on an estimate, but then she remembered the diploma above the rolltop desk.

"She graduated from secondary school in 1943," she said, after consulting the diploma, "so she would have been . . ."

"Around twelve in 1939," Sid finished.

Callie held the notebook reverently. It was so much more momentous when combined with the binoculars and the birding guides. Lady Whittington-Spence had been a birder. She had recorded her findings in this very notebook Callie held in her hands all these years later. She had learned from the booklets, which Sid was now looking at.

If Callie had been hoping the contents of the trunk would give her a clear way forward, it couldn't be more obvious. One disgruntled club leader was not going to keep her from birding.

"There are a bunch of these," Sid said. "Published between 1940 and 1943."

"This is amazing."

Sid dropped the book. Callie looked up to see what was wrong, but Sid was just sitting there, staring like she did. Was she bored by this? If you were always moving around the Scottish countryside, staying on castle grounds and living in trees, maybe some old books weren't that interesting.

Maybe it was immature to care about something like this. Callie tried to imagine, if she were still friends with Imogen, telling her about what she'd found in a magical trunk. She could imagine the scoffing. Imogen would have seen nothing interesting in an old dusty trunk. She definitely wouldn't have found super low-tech binoculars and a list of birds to be exciting.

"Pops has to see these," Sid said.

Or maybe Callie didn't know how to read other people at all.

But Ben had been napping when Sid left him, so they headed for the keep to show Callie's dad instead.

"Have you been to the top?" Sid asked as they approached the courtyard leading to the keep.

"My parents won't let me go inside at all. It's not structurally sound or whatever."

"Imagine how far you could see," Sid said. "Especially with those binoculars."

"Mom!" Callie called from right outside the keep. "Dad!"

There was no response. Callie considered. "I'm not inside if I stick my head in and yell up the stairs, right?"

Sid grinned.

Making absolutely sure to keep her feet technically outside the stone fortress, Callie leaned as far in as she could and shouted up into the darkness.

Moments later Callie and Sid could hear the sound of feet rushing down, even from outside.

"Callie!" Mom's face was bright red. Dad was right on her heels. "What's wrong?"

"Nothing." Before they could get angry that she'd scared them, Callie held the shoebox aloft. "But I found something amazing! We did."

Dad huffed and sat down on the steps. "Almost gave me a heart attack. You have strict orders not to come inside."

"I didn't. Sid watched. My feet stayed outside the whole time."

Mom narrowed her eyes at them both but took the shoebox and handed the lid to her husband. "Binoculars?"

"Not just binoculars!" Callie explained about the note-book, the birding booklets, how clearly she could see the starling tree across the water. "Did you know she was a birder? Lady Whittington-Spence?"

"Not that I can remember," Mom said. "Was she?"

Dad scrubbed a hand over his face. "Well, she did know birds by name. Remember? If you went on a walk, she'd point out the different breeds."

"Species," Callie corrected.

"That's true. And she had bird feeders in the garden," Mom added. "I remember her asking me to refill the seed when she didn't feel secure getting up on a ladder any-more."

"Which garden?" Callie asked. Weren't the whole grounds one giant garden?

"There was an enclosed garden, wasn't there? A rose garden, I think?"

Dad nodded. "On the northern edge of the property, maybe? I bet the leader of your birding club would be really interested to see these things, Cal."

"Oh. Yeah."

"Now I want to be clear with you girls that you should not go up in the keep at all. It's really not safe. We've got a lot of work to do up there."

"I know," Callie said. "You've told me a million times."

"Better safe than sorry." Dad stood up from the steps, his break over. "Hey, how did you end up getting into the trunk?"

"We unscrewed the hinges on the back. It was Sid's idea."

"You two make a good team," Mom said, with a totally embarrassing look that said *I'm so glad you're making a friend, my little misfit.*

"Okay, well, you guys get back to work," Callie said, packing the things into the shoebox and hurrying away from the keep before they could embarrass her any more.

"Why don't you want your parents to know you stopped going to the twitching club?" Sid asked as she caught up.

"It's complicated." Callie stopped and looked up at the cloudy sky. "Do you know which way is north?"

Without hesitation, Sid pointed beyond the castle in the opposite direction from the driveway. "I just don't get why they'd care. Are they super into birding or something?"

"What? Oh yeah. I mean, no. It's not the birding. It's just . . ."

Part of Callie wanted to tell Sid about the social requirement, and not only that but the whole reason she was homeschooling, the girls back home like starlings who could only move as a group and woe to the one who flew out of line.

But a bigger part of her didn't trust Sid all the way yet.

"Whoa," Sid said suddenly. "Is that . . . Can I have the binoculars?"

Grateful for the distraction, Callie handed them over and looked toward whatever had Sid so fascinated. High overhead, a black bird swooped in acrobatic rolls and tumbles through the air.

"It's a raven, isn't it?"

Sid shook her head and handed over the binoculars. "Take a closer look."

It was a sleek black bird, shaped like a raven. Its constant motion made it hard to see how it was different from the common Scottish bird that had visited Callie's window on her first night in the castle, and later haunted her chimney.

She shrugged. "I don't know."

"Come on." Sid took the binoculars back and set off at a run in the direction the bird was headed.

Callie, shoebox clasped to her chest, tried to keep up. "Where are we going?"

"We're going to see if it lands! So you can see better! Trust me, it's worth it."

Before Scotland, Callie had thought of bird-watching as something done by senior citizens in floppy hats and cargo pants. Her fifth-grade teacher had been a bird-watcher, and she'd been about ninety-seven years old.

But Mrs. Martinez and her bird-watching biddies would not have been able to race across the hilly grounds. They would have tripped on the sneaky roots and slipped on the wet grass. They would have stopped to rest on the curlicued iron benches and missed the birds entirely.

Finally Sid stopped. "There!" She brought the binoculars up to her eyes and gazed into a tall tree. She pulled Callie into the same spot she'd been standing in, handed her the binoculars, and pointed up into the shadows. "Look."

Callie looked. In theory, she should be able to see it better now that it was still. But it was a black bird, perched in the shadows of a dark tree. She was about to hand Sid the binoculars when she caught a flash of red. "Wait . . ."

She looked again. There it was, the raven-like bird, a bit smaller, but with the same glossy black feathers all over. The difference was, this bird had a long, thin, bright red beak and equally bright red legs.

"It's got a red beak," she said.

"Yes!" When Callie lowered the binoculars, Sid was grinning at her. "It's a red-billed chough! It's super rare."

"Really?"

"In Scotland, anyway," Sid said, pulling out her phone

and typing something into it. "And especially here on the east side."

"What's it called again?"

"Red-billed chough." Sid handed her phone over to Callie, open to an entry on a birding website.

Callie took the phone and sank down onto the grass, ignoring the damp as it soaked through her jeans. Her heart pounded from the sprint as she scanned the entry for the bird, which was a member of the same family as crows and ravens.

It was so like these common birds that Callie hadn't even been able to see the difference when it was in flight. It could blend in, if it wanted. If it was sleeping, feet tucked underneath its body and head tucked under its wing, no one would be able to see the difference.

But it was different. When you saw the bird fully, who it really was, it was dramatically different. Rare meant special to birders, but it seemed to Callie it might also mean lonely. If there were very few of these birds around, did this bird on the other side of the binoculars have any companions of its own kind? Did it need any to survive? How had it found itself here, on the wrong side of a country where it was already unusual?

As though satisfied Callie had gotten a good view, the red-billed chough let out a screechy caw and took off. Sid and Callie watched the bird wing its way toward the horizon.

"I wonder if your Lady Philippa ever spotted one of those," Sid said.

Callie thought of the long list of bird species in the leather journal and hugged the box to her chest. "I'll find it in her journal, if she did."

21 September 1939

Inverness

As the chickens inspired me, I figure they may
as well be the key to my escape. Not literally—
if only they could simply fly me out of here.
No, I decided they might be the best way to
get myself punished out of here. If Mrs Miller
thinks screaming in the middle of the night is
a disruption worthy of terrible punishment, she'll
see how much disruption I can cause with the
help of some feathered friends.

    After dinner, I pleaded headache when
everyone else went to play games. Mrs Miller
allowed me my "headache," probably trying to avoid
another Anagrams debacle. Rather than hide in the
bedroom, I went out to visit the girls in the
coop. I decided that it was too chilly for such
valuable members of the household—after all, we
rely on their eggs!—to remain in the drafty coop!
Instead I carried them, one by one, into the
house and up the back stairs, and deposited them
in Mrs Miller's bedroom.

    Now I'm waiting on my cot for a squawk
that's louder than the rest.

CHAPTER FIFTEEN

The next time the twitching club was supposed to meet, Callie rode her bike into town. After the thrill of spotting the red-billed chough with Sid, she understood why someone like Lady Philippa had spent so much time carefully recording the birds she spotted. And Callie wasn't going to let a roaster like Mr. Hunt keep her from something she wanted to do.

Callie had never cared about birds. Aside from seagulls, she had no idea what other birds were common in California. The California quail was the state bird; she remembered that from elementary school. But there had to be more than seagulls and quails.

Now, in this place where everything was new, there was something indescribable about seeing a new bird, a species she'd never seen before, and identifying it, and recording that moment in time. Maybe, years from now, she'd still remember the moment when she'd been walking away from the keep and Sid had spotted the raven-like bird with the bright red beak, and they'd taken off running across the hills until they finally reached the bird's destination and Callie had seen the red-billed chough for the first time.

Maybe she'd remember that as one of the first moments of their lifelong friendship. Or maybe she'd remember it as one of the only moments they ever shared together. Still, she'd remember it.

She parked her bike outside the library, took a steadying breath, and went in.

"Callie!" Esme exclaimed. "I'm so glad to see you back."

Callie stopped to look at the rainbow display Esme was arranging. "There's a new Lumberjanes?"

"Yep!" Esme handed it to her. "See anything else you want?"

"I don't want to mess up the display. It looks so nice."

"The saddest sight in the world is a perfect, untouched library display," Esme said. "Take whatever you like."

"Okay. I'll pick a couple more on my way out."

Esme smiled. "Are you giving twitching another go, then?"

Callie nodded. "Sort of. Thanks for the book." She headed for the stairs. Then, instead of going down to the meeting room, she headed up to the cozy area for kids. There were a few uniformed schoolkids on the upper level, plus a couple of moms chatting while their toddlers gnawed on picture books.

Callie settled at a table by herself and pulled Lady Philippa's birding journal and a guidebook from the Spence Castle library out of her bag. She set the guidebook aside and ran her hand over the worn leather cover of the journal. Even Imogen would have to admit this was seriously cool. Or even if she didn't, who cared what Imogen thought? Not Callie. Not anymore.

She opened it carefully and looked at the inside cover, where the girl who would become Lady Whittington-Spence had written her name in neat handwriting: *Philippa Spence, 1939.*

After a few pages of journal entries, a new page began in the same handwriting, covered in neat columns of bird species, dates and times of sightings, and notes about the behavior of the birds.

Pippa's Birds

Species	Date/Time
Red Crossbill	21/3/41 early morning
Ruffed Grouse	21/3/41 early morning
Short-Eared Owl	23/3/41 just after supper
Mourning Dove	24/3/41 midday
Storm Petrel	26/3/41 early afternoon
Black-Capped Chickadee	1/4/41 just after breakfast!

Location	Notes
The tallest conifer by the north gate	yellowish coloring indicates female, feeding on a conifer
On the path to the road	Funniest noise, like an engine failing to start, short crest, dull colors—female or juvenile?
Flying low across the front lawn	Heavily streaked, dark eye patches. Located its nest on the ground behind the stables—6 eggs
Perched on the tallest turret of the keep. Only got a clear view by using my new binoculars!	Its call is the saddest thing! No wonder they are called MOURNING doves!
Sailing on the Firth of Forth with Auntie Rebecca & Uncle Silas	Fluttering, batlike flight, black with a striking white band under its wings & at its rump
MY HAND!!! Out by the Italian fountain	I went out to fill the feeders with seed, and this bird hopped closer and closer. I held some seed in my palm and he hopped right up!

The list went on and on. Red kite, great skua, corncrake, osprey, starling. Lady Whittington-Spence—Pippa—had seen the very same starlings as Callie had. Well, not the same birds obviously, unless they lived a superlong time. But the same kind of birds in the very same tree, viewed from the same bedroom window where Callie perched at night.

Had Pippa related to the starlings' social nature? Or had she envied it?

Curious now about the lifespan of starlings, Callie looked through the stack of yellowed *Bird News and Notes* booklets. One issue had starlings on the cover, and inside, a feature described pertinent facts and behaviors and showed sketches of the birds from multiple angles and at multiple stages of development. Starlings, the book said, lived an average of three years.

"You are still interested in birds, then?" Esme slipped into the seat across from Callie. "But not the club."

Callie shrugged. "I guess I'm better on my own."

"I always thought group projects were rubbish. What have you got there?" She picked up a booklet. "These aren't ours, are they?"

Callie slid the stack of booklets across to Esme. "No, I found them in an old trunk at the castle."

Esme looked at one of the covers and whistled. "Wow, 1939. That's a collector's item there. I don't suppose you'd want to show Mr. Hunt."

Callie wrinkled her nose and shook her head.

"Fair." Esme started to go, then sat back down again. "You know, there's a birder you should check out. I think you'd like what she has to say. Her name is Mya-Rose Craig."

Callie looked up, waiting for more, but Esme only nodded at Pippa's journal. "Is that also from the trunk?"

"Not the trunk, but I found it in my room at the castle. It belonged to Lady Whittington-Spence. When she was my age."

"Wow. May I?"

Callie handed it to Esme, who looked carefully at the name on the inside, and the list Callie had been examining. Then she began to flip through to see what was in the later pages.

"Whoa." Callie reached out and stopped the pages so the journal opened onto something completely different from the list. "Look at that."

This looked much more like the pages in *Bird Notes and News*: sketches of a bird from different angles, with the whole page filled in with notes in the same handwriting as *Pippa's Birds* and the list in the front.

"'Western capercaillie,'" Esme read, "'also known as the wood grouse or heather cock.'"

The drawings weren't expert level, but they were detailed and much better than Callie could do. She came around to Esme's side of the table to look at the diagram and all its labels.

It looked like a cross between a chicken and a peacock. The body feathers were labeled as dark gray, and the breast feathers were labeled as metallic green. The bird had feathered legs and a tail fanning out like a peacock's, but without the distinctive eye patterns.

Around the sketches, Pippa had scrawled various notes: *observed eating bilberries, blueberries, and insects; in flight, wings make an enormous ruckus; bright red spot above each eye.*

"I hadn't seen the drawings yet," Callie said.

Esme thumbed through the rest of the journal. There were loads more sketches. "Then I'd say you've made an important discovery today."

Callie headed out of the library with a backpack weighed down by books from the rainbow display, more birding books from the nonfiction section, and Pippa's treasures. Any unease she'd felt about being kicked out of the official club and neglecting to tell her parents had vanished. She would still go to the library to learn about birding. There'd be other kids there. She might not really talk to any of them, but it wasn't like Mr. Hunt encouraged much talking during official meetings either.

"Oi, Callie!"

She was fastening the helmet Dad had brought home the day before—"Better safe than sorry!"—when Raj came out of the library, binoculars in hand.

"Aye, I thought that was you."

"Oh, hi," she said, getting on her bike.

"I heard about what happened. I'm sorry Mr. Hunt's such a git."

"A complete bowfin roaster," Callie said. "Where were you last week?"

"Home. Mum said I looked a bit peely-wally."

"Um, what?"

"You know, peely-wally."

"I . . . can't even guess what that means?"

Several of the other twitching club boys burst out of the library.

"Oi, look!" one of them shouted. "It's Princess Spence!"

"Where were you today?" another said as they approached Callie and Raj. "Mr. Hunt missed you!"

"Shut it, Silas," Raj said, but so quietly only Callie heard.

"Oi, Frodo, you coming or not? I can't destroy you in FIFA if you're not there."

"Sod off," Raj said with a grin. "I'll be along."

Right when Callie had been starting to think about showing Pippa's journal to Raj. Asking him to help her decipher the list and the notes. But if he could be friends with these guys, that was definitely not going to happen.

Callie adjusted her helmet. "See you around," she said to Raj, and then kicked off.

The quiet dignity of her departure was marred, however, by the sudden squeal of car brakes as a car coming around a corner nearly smashed into Callie head-on.

"Other side of the road, Princess!" one boy shouted.

"Sorry about her," another called to the car. "She's American!"

Callie waited, humiliated, for her heart to stop pounding out of control so she could cross to the other side of the road, trying her best to ignore the hoots and laughs from the boys, forcing herself not to look and see if Raj was joining in the laughter. Of course he would be. Those boys were his friends, and she was not Venetia Charles. She wasn't Pippa Worthington-Spence.

She might live in a castle, but she was still just awkward Callie.

22 September 1939

Inverness

My neck is tweaked, there are feathers in my hair, and I'll never get the smell of chicken poo out of my nostrils.

Upon discovering the chickens in her bedroom, Mrs Miller reacted with a great deal more dignity than when Magda poured ice water on my head. She appeared in the doorway to our shared room and calmly informed me that she needed some help. Then she led me to her room and asked if I had any idea how the chickens had gotten there.

Seeing as I was trying to get expelled from the house, I told Mrs Miller that I thought the chickens might be cold, and since our room was too full with five people but she was only one person, they might as well bunk with her. She nodded thoughtfully, asked me to please return them to the coop, and then, because I was clearly so concerned for the well-being of the chickens, she told me to SLEEP IN THE COOP WITH THEM!!!!

New plan: Write to Mother and tell her I'm being forced to sleep with animals!

Surely she'll come personally to remove me, and report Mrs Miller for good measure!

PS Of course the other girls all gathered round to watch as I was removing the chickens from Mrs Miller's bedroom. Ruby offered to help, but Mrs Miller wouldn't allow it. As I removed the final chicken, I'm not certain, but I almost think I saw a glint in Magda's eyes that looked something like . . . respect?

CHAPTER SIXTEEN

There was no time to lick her wounds; Callie was greeted at home by chaos. Mom was shouting something from the kitchen, Dad was running up the stairs, and Jax was standing in the entryway, sobbing.

"Jaxy, what's wrong?!"

"I thought it would have a fun ride!" he sobbed.

Since there was no guessing where Dad was sprinting, Callie headed for the kitchen. She found Mom with her head stuck inside a cupboard. Cabinet? Some sort of hole in the wall. She was talking in the soothing voice she used to calm Jax down from nightmares.

"It's all right," she cooed into the empty space. "You're going to be fine."

"Mom?"

She jumped, and her head banged into the top of the cupboard. "Oh, jeez, Callie, you scared me."

"Sorry. What's going on? Jax is losing his mind in the entryway."

"Jax should have thought things through before he put Mr. Collywobbles in the dumbwaiter."

"I'm sorry, what?"

Right then, Mom's phone pinged with a text. "Read that for me, would you?" she said, sticking her head back inside the cupboard.

"It's from Dad. 'Not on the second floor.' What's not on the second floor?"

"Mr. Collywobbles. Okay, tell him to stay there and I'm going up to the third. You stay here, please."

Completely baffled, Callie watched her mom dash from the room. A moment later, Jax appeared, sniffling.

"Jaxy?" Callie spoke gently. "Who's Mr. Colly . . . wob?"

"Collywobbles," he sniffled. "She's our new cat."

"We have a cat? Named Mr. Collywobbles?"

Jax looked like he was about to burst into full-blown waterworks again, so Callie decided not to ask him any more questions. She turned to the cabinet where her mother had been talking to . . . nothing.

The space behind the door wasn't very deep—a foot at the most—and a couple of feet wide. But when Callie stuck her head inside, the space went down into darkness, like an elevator shaft, and up to the faraway bottom of a compartment on a pulley system.

It was a dumbwaiter! Callie had read about them in books. A way to deliver meals or other heavy items from one level to another, like a miniature elevator. Except too small for humans, even Jax.

Then it dawned on Callie what had happened. "You put the cat in the dumbwaiter?"

Jax nodded miserably.

"And . . . sent it to another floor?"

His eyes brimmed over with tears.

"Don't cry. I mean, cry if you want to. But the cat's going to be all right. It only went for a little ride, like you said."

Jax sank down on the couch and Callie stuck her head inside the dumbwaiter. "It's okay, kitty, kitty," she said into the darkness.

"Well," Mom said a few moments later, returning to the kitchen with Dad right behind her. "She's not on the second or third floor."

Callie frowned. "You didn't have time to check the entire floors."

"No, we checked the dumbwaiter cabinets on those floors. They have little latches on the outside. I don't think she would have been able to push her way out."

Callie stuck her head in the empty space again. The darkness went a long way up, like looking up from the bottom of an elevator shaft. On the right was a rope like the ones in the school auditorium, used for pulling the heavy black drapes open and closed. "This moves the dumbwaiter up and down?"

She wrapped her hands around the thick ropes and was about to pull when Jax cried out, "Wait!"

Callie froze.

"What if Mr. Collywobbles is above or below the elevator and gets crushed when you move it?"

Callie took her hands off the ropes. She could see from looking up the shaft that the cat wasn't below the compartment, but Jax had a point. It probably wasn't the best idea to move the mechanical contraption when they had no idea where the cat was.

"When did we get a cat?" she asked.

Mom shook her head and Dad let out a shaky laugh. "Funny story, really. One of Jax's classmates had a litter of kittens at the school pickup line. They were looking for homes, and I thought, considering the mice around here . . ."

"It's a kitten? Lost in the castle?"

Jax whimpered.

Right then Sid passed by on her bike, outside the kitchen.

"Hang on." Callie raced to the window and banged on

it to catch Sid's attention, motioning for her to stop. If she knew her parents, they weren't going to take this seriously, and she was going to need more than Jax for help to track down the kitten. Callie met Sid at the front door. "Can you come in and help with something?"

"Need to bust into another mysterious trunk?" Sid said with a smile. "I'm all out of keys."

Callie explained the crisis as she led Sid into the kitchen.

"How's she going to help?" Jax asked.

Sid didn't answer. She looked bored, staring out the window.

"She knows about . . . nature stuff," Callie said, suddenly feeling sort of sheepish. Why *had* she dragged Sid into this? "Sorry, you don't have to help if you don't want to. Sid?"

Sid waved Callie off and walked over to the cabinet. "What level is the dumbwaiter on right now?"

"Second floor," Dad said, clearly regretting the adorable impulse pet he'd acquired that afternoon.

"Show me where?" Sid said to Callie.

"I'll let you guys handle this," Mom said. "I've got to finish the dining room molding today if I'm going to stay on track."

Jax's lip trembled. This was an all-hands-on-deck emergency! How could Mom abandon them, like the kitten's life wasn't on the line?! But this was exactly what Callie knew would happen.

"Don't worry, Jaxy," she said. "You stay here and listen for meows, okay?"

Glad for a task, Jax nodded gravely, and Callie led Sid to the stairs. "Third door on the right," Dad called after them.

"What's your plan?" Callie asked.

"I don't actually know. But I want to see how it might have gotten out of the compartment. The stairs aren't rotten anymore!"

Callie grinned as Sid took the now-sturdy stairs two at a time. "I know. My mom has been working super hard."

"My mum was handy like that," Sid said. "More metal-work than woodwork, though."

It was a bread crumb. Sid had known her mother.

"Did she . . . teach you how to do any of that?"

Sid was quiet for a moment. They reached the top of the stairs. "No," she finally said.

The third room on the right was across the hall from Callie's bedroom. Like most of the rooms, it had been kept closed up, since no one was using it. Callie pushed the door open and together they stepped into the musty room.

Sid went straight to the heavy curtains and tugged them open, coughing at the dust that had been building for decades. Light streamed in, illuminating the dust, but also the beautiful carvings on the ceiling, and bookshelves, and a massive desk in the center of the room. It was like her own personal library, steps away from her bedroom.

"Seems weird to put a library where the dumbwaiter goes," Sid said. "Unless whoever used this room worked constantly and had their meals sent up."

Could it have been Pippa? Of course, there had been many other members of the Whittington-Spence family over many generations. It could have been anyone. Callie needed to do more research. On so many things.

"Here it is." Sid found a waist-high cabinet door, undid the latch, and opened it up.

Callie wished fervently that a frazzled kitten might tumble straight into Sid's arms. But no such luck. It was an empty cupboard, nothing more. The only thing that made it different from any other cupboard was the pulley system that could move it up and down to different levels.

Sid felt around inside the cabinet. "Yep," she finally said. "Feel this."

Callie felt along the top front edge of the cupboard where Sid's hands were. There was a gap between the miniature elevator and the wall. "It's only a couple of inches. Could a cat really get through?"

"A kitten could, for sure. The lady we worked for last summer had a whole bunch of cats, and they were forever squeezing into the most ridiculous places."

"So you think . . . what? It climbed on top of the moving compartment thing?"

"Possible." She grabbed the ropes. "I'm going to move it a little, so we can see if it's on top."

Callie knew Jax would freak out down in the kitchen when he saw the ropes moving, but she'd let Dad deal with that. Sid had a plan; she was cool under pressure.

The pulley system creaked as the dumbwaiter moved down far enough to see that there was nothing on top of the compartment. Nothing except kitten-size pawprints in decades' worth of dust.

"Yes!" Callie held up both hands, which Sid met in a double high five. "I mean . . . sort of. At least we know she was here."

"Yeah. But where did she go next?"

The chute was long and dark. There was nowhere else the kitten could have gone. If she'd been on top of the compartment, she couldn't have fallen down; there wasn't enough space for her to slip through, no matter how tiny she was.

"Maybe there are, like . . . tunnels? That branch off or something?"

Sid nodded. "Like ducts for heating, or plumbing?"

That was a logical reason for tunnels. Callie preferred to think of them as secret passageways between the walls of a castle. *Her* castle. There were no tunnels at their eye level, but the dumbwaiter would have stopped farther up. Which meant the tunnels might be farther up.

"Can you lower it a little more?" Callie asked.

Sid didn't even ask why; she just did it.

When the compartment was low enough, Callie leaned way in to look up. She thought she might see something, but her angle was weird, leaning in and twisting up in the small space. It wasn't so small her body wouldn't fit, though.

"Do you think it'll hold my weight?" she asked.

Sid's eyes went wide. "No."

Callie sighed. It had probably been a stupid idea anyway. Except right then they heard the unmistakable sound of a kitten. A terrified kitten.

"Okay," Sid said. "We have to move the desk. Over here, in front of the dumbwaiter."

Callie paused. Sid had trusted her, so she was trusting Sid. The desk was massive, and at first Callie thought it must be bolted into the floor, except Sid pointed out that the floor was stone, so that was probably impossible. With much grunting and heaving and sweating, they finally got the desk against the wall. It was right at the same level as the dumbwaiter.

"Now what?" Callie asked. Sid had started clearing the books and knickknacks and dusty lamp off the desk, so Callie helped.

"Now," Sid said, wiping a dirty hand across her sweaty forehead, leaving a grimy streak behind. "This will hold your weight. And I can hold on to your legs just in case. I think you should be able to stand on this . . ."

"But squeeze my body into the shaft and reach the tunnel."

"Exactly."

This was a lot for a kitten Callie didn't know. She didn't even really like cats, honestly. Then it mewled again, more pitifully, if that was possible.

"I can do it, if you want," Sid said.

"No. This is for my brother."

Callie climbed onto the desk, and Sid climbed up next to her, ready to clamp onto her legs to avert disaster. Callie edged herself right up next to the opening. First she leaned into the shaft on all fours, leaving her knees on the desk but testing her weight on the dumbwaiter with her hands. So far, so good.

As though cheering her on, the kitten cried again.

The inside of the chute was rough stone, so Callie found a handhold and pulled herself up, with much scraping and some words she wasn't allowed to say in front of Jax, but finally, awkwardly, she was half standing, half leaning upright in the chute, with her feet still on the desk.

It was pitch-dark inside the chute, and cold. Callie's chest was tight, whether from dust or impending panic. But the cries were louder now, and Callie only had to feel around for a moment before she found an opening that was definitely kitten-size.

"Hey, Mr. Collywobbles," she said into the darkness.

"Mew."

"I'm sure you're scared. I don't blame you. This morning you were safe with your mama and your brothers and sisters, and now you're here in this weird place."

"Mewwww."

"But look, we're going to take good care of you. I promise."

She was kind of hoping the kitten would leap into her arms and she could avoid stretching her hands into blackness that could contain rodents or spiders or any number of monsters. Suddenly secret passageways inside a castle did not sound nearly as cool.

"MEWWWLLLL."

Callie sighed. "Okay, Mr. C. I'm reaching in. You better not bite." Though if a kitten bite was the worst thing that happened to her up in this spooky, dusty confined space, she would be totally grateful.

"Do you see it?" Sid called up from Callie's feet.

"I can't see anything," Callie said. "But I think I'm right in front of it! Hang on."

She had come this far. She took a deep breath and stuck her arms into the opening. At first she felt only shuddery things like spiderwebs and little crunchy things she desperately hoped were bugs and not bones of some sort. She pressed her cheek against the stone wall in front of her so she could lean another inch farther in, and finally her fingers brushed something fuzzy and warm.

"Please don't be a rat, please don't be a rat," she chanted as she gently wrapped her hands around it and pulled it toward her. The kitten froze at first, but as soon as Callie pulled it from the opening and cradled it to herself, the kitten melted into her and mewled one more time.

"Got it," she called to Sid.

Getting out proved to be even more awkward than getting in, trying not to smoosh the tiny kitten cradled in her arms, but finally Callie and the kitten were out of the chute and sitting on the massive desk. "She's shaking," Callie said.

"She only needs to warm up." Sid stroked the kitten's head with a single finger. "You were really brave."

Callie thought Sid was talking to the kitten. But then she glanced up and found Sid looking at her. "Thanks. I couldn't have done it without you."

* * *

Curled up on the hearth next to the fire, Mr. Collywobbles seemed like she'd never been in any danger. The humans sprawled around the kitchen looked like they'd been through a war.

"Just so we're clear, Jaxy," Dad said from the kitchen table, where he was slumped with his head in his hands. "Do not put Mr. Collywobbles in the dumbwaiter again."

"Don't put *anything* in the dumbwaiter again," Mom amended.

Now that Mr. Collywobbles had returned none the worse for wear, Jax had completely forgotten his misery.

"It's okay," he whispered to the cat, scratching behind her ears. "We'll go on other adventures."

"No adventures," both parents said together.

"Well, I'm right glad it all worked out," Ben said. He'd shown up after Callie and Sid had gone upstairs, wondering where his granddaughter had gotten off to when he was expecting her back at the cottage. "Before I go, though, might I . . . might I ask about the name?"

Callie and her parents shrugged, and all eyes turned to Jax.

"I like the word," he said. "My teacher says it when she turns us on the merry-go-round. That she's got the collywobbles. It's a jolly word."

Ben choked back a chuckle. "I see. Very original. Right, then, I'm off."

"What about the Mr. part?" Dad asked. "You do know she's a girl."

This time Jax shrugged. "It's just her name. Don't ask me."

Quietly, so Jax and Mr. Collywobbles wouldn't be bothered, Sid murmured to Callie, "It means nausea."

"What?"

"Collywobbles. It means nausea."

Callie looked around at her parents draped over the table, exhausted. She looked at Sid's grimy face and her own arms and legs covered in soot and decades of dust. She thought of the feeling in her stomach when she had realized that with one wrong move, she and the kitten could have fallen to their very dramatic deaths.

"That . . . sounds about right," she said.

28 September 1939

Inverness

While Operation: Chicken Infestation didn't get me kicked out of here, it did get me Magda's grudging respect: I'm almost sure of it. When there are things I don't know or understand about living simply and without servants, she almost never pokes fun anymore. She definitely delights in knowing things I don't, don't get me wrong, but she doesn't make me feel like such a fool when she sets me straight.

One thing she cannot seem to teach me is how to sleep through the racket of four other girls in one cramped room. And to top it off, there are pigeons roosting on a ledge outside our window. Also, they make a horrible racket, far too early in the morning.

The upside of lying awake for hours is that it gives me plenty of time to brainstorm my next move. I'm losing faith in my ability to get kicked out, however. If setting a brood of chickens loose in Mrs Miller's room wasn't going to do it, I'm not sure what would. At least, if I'm not willing to cause actual harm, which I'm not.

I'm not Mother.

Last night when I was complaining about the pigeons, Magda said it was kind of special to be able to look out the window and watch baby pigeons. According to her, you never see baby pigeons out and about like you see ducklings or goslings or chicks, because baby pigeons stay in the nest until they are fully grown. Like humans, Bea said, and then everyone was silent. (Apart from the pigeons.)

Because here we are, not fully grown, yet out of our nests long before we ought to be.

When Magda finally fell asleep, I thought I was the only one left awake. But then I heard Rosie's tiny voice.

"I know something else about pigeons," she said.

I waited, unsure if she meant to tell me or only lord her knowledge over me. Finally I said, "What is it?"

She said, "Pigeons can find their way home from one thousand miles away. So maybe we'll make it home too."

CHAPTER SEVENTEEN

"Why do we have to haul all these up to the top floor?" Sid asked, looking at the pile of birding books on a table on the nonfiction level of the library.

Callie eyed the door to the meeting room. At any moment, Mr. Hunt and the birding club could emerge. "It's cozier up there," she said, taking half the stack in her arms and heading for the stairs.

Sid grumbled behind her, all the way up. But once they were seated on beanbags upstairs, she looked around and said, "Okay, you're right. This is much cozier."

Callie grinned and opened the guide to British birds on the top of the stack.

"I suppose there's no point asking why we don't just use the Internet to search for these birds?" Sid said, opening another giant field guide.

"Nope," Callie said. She'd already explained this to Sid. Pippa wouldn't have had the Internet in 1939. She wouldn't have had birding apps. It felt like cheating somehow to use them now.

But Callie had used the Internet to look up Mya-Rose Craig, the birder Esme had mentioned. She was surprised to find out Mya-Rose was young. An older teen now, but she'd been blogging about birds and entering competitions since she was younger than Callie. And Mya-Rose wasn't only a birder—she was outspoken about the sexism in birding. She's come up against rule-sticklers who wouldn't count female birds. And worse, she'd been ignored and belittled and discounted simply for being a girl in the boy-heavy activity.

Mya-Rose hadn't let it stop her, and Callie wasn't going to either.

"Okay, so look at this." Sid pushed a book in front of Callie. It was open to a page with the header *Shorebirds* and illustrations of a bunch of different birds. "See how a lot of them have the same general body shape? Long, thin legs, for wading. A longish bill? That's for poking into the water or sand to find food."

Sid had wanted to show Callie how certain traits like

body shape, or behaviors, like what a bird ate, could help her immediately narrow down what family a bird might be in, which would then make it easier to figure out a bird's specific species. "Calliope?"

Callie's head snapped up at the sound of Mr. Hunt's voice. What was he doing here on the top level of the library? She could almost guarantee he was not a fan of children's books.

"Esme told me I'd find you up here," he said.

Behind him, Esme peeked her head around and mouthed, *Sorry*.

"It's Callie, actually."

He raised an eyebrow but went on, undaunted. "If you will recall, we discussed the possibility of the birding club doing an excursion on the grounds of Spence Castle. Did you ask your parents' permission, as promised?"

Callie blinked at this insufferable man. "You kicked me out of the club."

"Yes, well, I think it was clear to all involved that you were not exactly a match for a serious twitching club."

Esme stepped into full view. "Actually, these girls look like quite serious twitchers," she said, indicating their stacks of field guides.

Callie was starting to feel ridiculous, slumped down low on a beanbag while Mr. Hunt and his ramrod posture towered over her.

"Thank you, Esme," she said, climbing to her feet. "No, Mr. Hunt, I decided the grounds of Spence Castle wouldn't be the right match for your club's excursion."

Sid snickered behind Callie. "It's too bad," she said. "They probably would have loved to see the red-billed chough."

"There's a red-billed chough at Spence?" Mr. Hunt spluttered. After a moment's consideration, he awkwardly folded himself down onto the ground and motioned for Callie to return to her beanbag.

"I'm terribly sorry for our previous misunderstanding, Calliope. Callie," he said. "You must understand—it's our club's year to host the regional Big Day youth birding competition. I'd planned to host it at Loch Leven, but they've closed it for several weeks, so as not to disrupt some endangered gray wagtails who are presently nesting. The Spence grounds would be perfect, frankly, as a large acreage with clear boundaries and a variety of arboreal density and vegetation."

Callie stared at him. She wasn't about to ask what he was talking about.

"You are, of course, welcome to return to the club," he said when she didn't immediately bow to his wishes. "And even count the females, if you so wish."

"Magnanimous of you, Henry," Esme said under her breath.

He had some nerve. Offering her membership in his stupid, sexist club, like that would entice her to give him what he wanted? But thoughts were coming together in Callie's head like a bird's nest—wispy bits of twigs and twine, but put together they made a cozy home. A fortress.

She might not have been able to say what she said next if it hadn't been for Esme offering her encouragement behind Mr. Hunt, and Sid's quiet certainty next to her. But they were there, and she was not alone.

"I don't want to be in your club," Callie said, and Esme nodded in approval. "And I don't need your permission to count female birds."

Mr. Hunt huffed and climbed to his feet. "I'm sorry you feel that way—"

"But you can have your day at the castle—my parents will say yes—and we'll be there." She linked arms with Sid. "We'll be competing as our own club, and we'll be counting whatever birds we like. Will you have a problem with that?"

Mr. Hunt's ears had gone red while Callie was speaking, and now his face followed. "Young lady, you can't simply declare yourself a club! You don't seem to understand there are rules and regulations—"

"All right, Henry," Esme said, taking his arm and guiding him toward the stairs. "I think that sounds like an awfully generous offer. Just remember: red-billed . . ."

Esme turned back to the girls with a questioning look.

"Chough," Sid supplied.

"Red-billed chough," Esme cooed, leading Mr. Hunt down the stairs.

As soon as they were gone, Callie turned to Sid. "What's a Big Day competition?"

Sid shook her head. "You went all tough negotiator and you didn't even know what you were negotiating?"

"I know I want to beat that guy at his own game, only playing by my own rules. Don't you?"

"So basically," Callie told her parents at dinner that night, "Mr. Hunt's club, plus some other youth clubs from the area, would all come to the grounds for one day. And within that day, each team would be trying to identify as many different species as possible."

"That sounds like fun!" Mom said.

Jax wrinkled his nose. "They just . . . look for birds? All day long?"

"I think it sounds great," Dad said. "You tell this Mr. Hunt to name the day! Or should I swing by the next time you go to a meeting?"

"No!" Callie said. "That's fine. He's very . . . focused during meetings. I'll tell him. Thank you."

Her parents beamed at her. Callie felt the tiniest prick of guilt, misleading them, but the thought of besting Mr. Hunt took over soon enough.

Callie was up and walking the grounds earlier than usual the next morning. Crested larks could be seen throughout the day, but the crests on their heads stood up when they sang, and they sang most often in the mornings. There was no guarantee she would find any on the castle grounds, but Pippa had found some in 1942. So it was definitely possible.

Callie was more motivated than ever. Mya-Rose's blog had led her to more articles about women in birding. It turned out women had been active in birding since the beginning, starting with Harriet Lawrence Hemenway and Minna Hall. In the 1890s, they organized a boycott to stop the slaughter of birds for their feathers, used in fashionable hats, and ended up getting landmark conservation laws passed, which led to the formation of the still-active National Audubon Society, a massive bird-focused conservation organization in the United States.

But even though women had started the Audubon Society, and women still made up 72 percent of the membership, the staff running the organization was 75 percent male. And in 115 years, the organization had never had a female president.

Callie wasn't setting out to be the president of the Audubon Society, at least not yet, but the more practice she got before the Big Day, the better position she'd be in to do well for Mr. Hunt's competition. And she had the literal home field advantage. She could scope out as many regular nesting spots as possible, and then she'd know exactly where to find certain birds when the time came.

She would have invited Sid to join her, but it was too early in the morning to knock on the cottage door. Ben tended to be up with the sun, but Callie had a feeling Sid slept in as late as she wanted to. Which made it even more of a shock when Sid fell out of a tree directly in front of Callie.

"Sid!"

It had been a low branch. Callie expected Sid to sit up with a sheepish laugh. But she didn't. She lay on the ground. Her eyes were open but staring into nothing, like so many times before. But this was different. Her whole body was stiff and her arms and legs jerked, almost like she was having a nightmare.

"Oh my gosh," Callie breathed, kneeling at Sid's side. "Help!" she called. Sid's grandfather could be anywhere on the property. She should probably run back to the castle and get her parents, but that would take time, and Callie didn't want to leave Sid alone in this state.

She didn't have to. Ben appeared moments later,

taking off his jacket and wedging it under his grand-daughter's head.

"What's happening? Should I call an ambulance?" Callie didn't even know how to call an ambulance in Scotland. Was it 911, like at home?

Ben looked at his watch. "Not just yet, lassie." He was totally calm, like Sid had gotten a paper cut, rather than fallen out of a tree with convulsions. "Could you move that rock away from her knee so she doesn't bang into it?"

Callie moved the rock, her heart pounding.

"She has epilepsy," Ben went on, still completely calm. "Seizures happen. We wait it out, protect her head, and she'll be all right."

"She fell." Callie knew Sid wasn't supposed to climb trees, but this seemed like important information. Drool trickled from the side of Sid's mouth.

Ben grimaced and looked up into the tree above them. After another moment, the convulsions died down. The old gardener rolled Sid over onto her side. She began to cough, spitting out saliva.

"All right, old girl," he said, stroking her back. "You're all right. I'm here. I'm always here."

"I'm here too," Callie said, but Sid didn't register her presence. She looked like she'd just woken up. "Is this . . . does this happen a lot?"

"Seizures happen a lot," the gardener said. Now that

his granddaughter was all right, he looked shaken, like he'd used up all his calm in getting her through it. "But for Cressida, they don't usually look like that."

"Sid," she mumbled.

A smile spread across his weathered face. "*Sid* has something called juvenile absence epilepsy. Her seizures usually look more like she's spaced out for a minute. A few seconds, even. She doesn't fall, or shake, but her brain is busy doing something else."

"When she looks like she's not listening . . . ?"

"Aye, that's a seizure. Course, there are definitely times she's plain not listening to me, or she wouldn't be climbing in trees when she oughtn't. But I know she listens to you. Never stops talking about you, really."

Callie flushed. All those times Callie had thought Sid was ignoring her or didn't care what she was saying, maybe that hadn't been the case at all.

"Absence seizures happen multiple times a day," Ben said. "It's why some things that seem like normal activities are dangerous for her. Because if a seizure hits when she's in the middle of something . . . well, this is a perfect example. I'd wager she lost her balance because of an absence seizure. Then the impact of the fall brought on this more obvious kind."

So much about Sid was starting to make sense. Not only the way she blanked out sometimes, but the way she was always on guard, hesitant to let Callie in. "She's always had this?"

"Came on a couple of years ago. But her mum had the same thing, so I'm an old pro. My daughter was just like her, always ignoring the rules and doing what she wanted."

"I'm right here," Sid said, starting to look more like herself again. Herself, but embarrassed.

"I'm glad you're okay," Callie offered.

"Cressida," Ben said in the sharpest tone Callie had heard from him. "You were right lucky your friend was here. The fall alone could have injured you badly. No trees. No risks."

Sid nodded dutifully. "I'm sorry, Pops."

He grunted and got to his feet, taking his dirt-covered jacket with him. "You'll be the death of me, lass."

Callie had a million questions as he walked away, but one look at Sid and she knew Sid would be the death of her if she asked any of them.

"Um," she said, looking down at her binoculars. "I'm trying to find a crested lark. Any idea where they might be?"

3 October 1939

Inverness

There's a tall, grey-blue bird that stands in the pond just over the hill. It's large, with long spindly legs and a bill like a dagger. When I told Mrs Miller it has a dramatic black stripe across its eye, she told me it must be a great blue heron. She said they're not common around these parts, but then neither are most of us in this house.

I saw it one day when I was wandering the grounds and stopped to watch for a while. It stood there, never moving. The next day, I saw it again, but this time I waited, and finally I saw it catch a fish with a lightning-flash stab into the water.

I've been to see it most days since, even though the weather's gotten awful and Mrs Miller says I mustn't linger out of doors or I'll catch my death of cold. I'm more likely to catch my death of boredom, but I didn't say so because Mother told me I had to be very courteous to these people who are opening their homes to war evacuees.

Not that Mother has shown me the common

courtesy of responding to my letter in which I told her the state of things here.

I generally wait until Mrs Miller is busy with one of the other children, and I slip out. The heron is always there, and unlike so many of the other birds I see around the grounds, he's always alone.

I guess I don't know he's a he. But he feels very stoic, rather like Father.

I wonder if he chooses to be alone, or if he simply doesn't know how to relate to the other birds.

CHAPTER EIGHTEEN

By the day of the birding competition, Callie and Sid had scouted every inch of the Spence Castle grounds. When she'd laid down the gauntlet for Mr. Hunt, Callie hadn't actually believed she and Sid could beat his team, much less three other experienced youth teams from around Scotland, but she'd made her point by insisting on her own rules. That alone had been pretty brave.

Now, though, after a week of near nonstop birding with Sid, her confidence had soared. She knew these grounds. She knew about the ravine hidden behind the copse of trees on the east side of the property. She knew the crumbling wall on the south edge looked like the property boundary, but really it extended farther, far enough to include a haw-finch nest.

She had learned how bird-watching didn't always start when birders spotted a bird. Often they heard the birds first, hidden in the trees. Callie had never realized how distinct the different birdcalls were. But Sid could hear a call and say, "That's a willow warbler," or, "That's a common house martin."

Knowing the calls led to finding the birds, because Sid knew that a willow warbler builds its nest in low vegetation, close to the ground. So they'd head toward the call, but instead of scanning the trees, they'd look lower down.

Callie couldn't identify the birdcalls yet, but she was learning. And Sid got an app on her phone that would listen to a bit of a recorded birdcall and identify the species. For her own purposes, Callie thought the app was sort of cheating, since Pippa wouldn't have had anything of the sort. But using technology to learn basically counted as homeschooling, and for the Big Day, she was absolutely going to use any tool available.

Their long days of rambling the grounds and scanning the skies also meant Sid had opened up to Callie a little more, bit by bit. She said her grandfather wanted Callie to understand juvenile absence seizures if they were going to be spending a lot of time together. But Callie thought Sid might actually be glad to have someone to talk to about it.

When the seizures first started happening, Sid had been enrolled in a comprehensive school like the one in South Kingsferry. Ben was the resident landscaper on the grounds of a castle in the Highlands, and they'd lived in the same place for years. Sid had a group of friends and did well in school.

Callie tried to imagine fiercely independent Sid as one of a group of friends. Would she have been more of a leader, or a follower? Would she have stood up to Imogen?

But then she started having absence seizures. The thing about them, though, was that no one could tell she was having a seizure if she was sitting at a desk or a lunch table or doing her homework. Her brain would start misfiring and sending wonky messages, and when she came out of the seizure, she wouldn't even know what had happened.

More and more often, she missed a teacher's question, or important information being imparted about permission slips or homework or group projects. She fell behind in school, and worse, became convinced she was dumb and shouldn't even bother trying.

She got moved into remedial classes, away from her friends, who suddenly saw her as different. More than that, Sid's friends thought she had gotten standoffish or self-involved, that when she spaced out, she wasn't listening to them or didn't care. Which was exactly what Callie had thought too.

When Ben finally recognized the symptoms as the same ones Sid's mother had gone through, he got super protective. Sid's friends didn't understand why she kept turning down invitations to do things that wouldn't be safe for her. Ice-skating, swimming in the quarry—

"Using power tools?" Callie had asked.

"Well, yeah. I mean, no one ever offered that before you," Sid said. "But what if I checked out in the middle of using a dangerous tool like that?"

"But you never told them what was going on," Callie said. "They would have understood, wouldn't they? I do."

"Maybe. But it didn't happen overnight. By the time we'd figured out what was going on, the teachers already believed I wouldn't focus. My friends already believed I was stuck-up or whatever. People decide what they think of you, and then . . ."

"Yeah," Callie agreed. "Like if someone thinks you're a thief, it's going to be really super hard to gain their trust."

Sid shoved Callie in the shoulder and they both laughed. But then Sid grew somber again. "Pops is the only one I know for sure that I can always count on."

"You're certain you'll be all right?" Ben asked Sid for the millionth time as he heaved some tools into the back of his truck.

"She'll be fine." Mom put her arm around Sid's shoulder

and squeezed. "We'll treat her like one of our own."

Ben still looked skeptical. Everyone else just looked tired; up early for the start of the Big Day. Ben had an interview in Aberdeen for a new project that would start as soon as the Spence Castle grounds were finished. Normally, he'd bring Sid along. But it was the day of the competition, and Callie's parents had offered to watch Sid so she didn't have to go with him. (Even though Callie and Sid would be roaming the grounds all day and her parents wouldn't really be watching either of them.)

It wouldn't have been a big deal for almost anyone else. But it was easy to see how anxious Ben was about leaving his granddaughter. It had only ever been the two of them. "You'll check in with me?" he said, waving his phone. "Every hour?"

"Aye, Pops. And you'll check in with me? You're sure you're up to this?"

Ben narrowed his eyes at Sid. "Who's the adult here?"

"Thank you for letting her stay," Callie said. "I really need her for the competition."

Ben turned his gaze on Callie. "You remember what to do if . . . You get her on the ground safely. Nothing in her mouth. You roll her on her side when—"

"Pops," Sid groaned.

Callie knew. She remembered every second from when Sid had her first noticeable seizure. And since then, she'd researched all she could about juvenile absence epilepsy and learned more about what to do and what not to do to help her friend.

She held up a hand like she was making an oath. "I solemnly swear we shall climb no trees."

Ben laughed. "Right, then." He pressed a grateful hand into Callie's mom's. "I guess if I'm going to leave her with anyone, I could do worse than you folks."

"They're here!" Dad called from the front room, where he had a perfect view of the castle drive.

"You ready?" Sid said as she and Callie stood to gather their things—binoculars, Sid's phone, backpacks with snacks and water and field guides.

"So ready." Somewhere along the way this had gotten bigger than proving Mr. Hunt wrong. That was still part of it, sure, but an even bigger part of Callie had found something she cared about and believed in. She wanted to do this for Pippa. She wanted to make Esme proud. And more than anything else, she wanted to do it because she was doing it with Sid.

"I wanna come," Jax whined. Again.

"I've already told you, buddy, birders have to be super quiet."

"I'm quiet!" In frustration, Jax kicked the couch, which jostled the end table, which knocked over a lamp with a deafening crash of shattering glass.

Sid tried to stifle a laugh and failed.

Mom sighed. "Jaxy, get the dustpan and help me clean this up. You girls get on out there and greet your guests."

"Sorry, Jax," Sid said. "How about we take you birding another day?"

"Whatever," he said, trudging toward the broom closet. "Birds are stupid."

Out in front of the castle, a bunch of unfamiliar kids were piling out of a van. Dad was shaking hands with their leader, a man even older than Ben, with absolutely no hair and a T-shirt that said INVERNESS TWITCHERS.

"Welcome to Spence," Dad said, catching sight of Callie. "Come on over here, Callie-kins."

Callie was making the sort of awkward small talk adults always inflict on kids when another van rumbled across the gravel, this time with Mr. Hunt at the wheel.

"Henry, you old dunderheid!" the first leader exclaimed as Mr. Hunt climbed out of the van.

The twitching club boys piled out of the second van; Raj emerged last, scanning the people already gathered until he spotted Callie and waved.

"Go say hi to your friends," Dad said, urging Callie toward the boys who were definitely not her friends, and Raj, who maybe was but he was also their friend, so Callie didn't know what to think.

"Hey," Raj said, stepping away from the other boys. So at least he thought he was her friend. "This is cool of you, to let us do this here."

"I'm doing it too. With Sid." Callie looked over her shoulder, but Sid was standing off to the side, observing the youth birders like they were some sort of strange, unknown species.

"I wanted to say"—Raj scuffed the dirt with his toe—"I agree with you."

"About what?"

"The female birds. I wish I'd been there that day, to say so. But you're totally right."

"Thanks."

"And I'm sorry about those guys in the club. I know they seem awful."

"Why do they call you Frodo?"

Raj cringed. Then he gestured to himself. "I mean . . . because I'm short?"

"You're right," Callie said. "They do seem awful."

"I guess they are. It's just . . . I've known them forever. And I have to go to school with them, you know?"

Callie did know. She'd stood by when Imogen picked on defenseless kids. She'd stood by when Imogen picked on her. These things weren't simple.

She caught Sid's eye and waved her over. "This is Sid. She lives in the cottage."

Raj gave Sid a nod.

"This is Raj. He's the only one in Mr. Hunt's club who isn't an absolute roaster."

Sid and Raj looked from Callie to each other and then burst into laughter.

"What? Did I use that wrong?"

"No," Sid gasped. "But it sounds dead funny, coming from you."

"Well," Callie said. "You can both . . . go boil your heads!"

That set off an even more explosive round of laughter that earned glares from Mr. Hunt as he made his way to the front steps of the castle and two more vans pulled up the castle drive.

"Attention, please," Mr. Hunt said, the moment the van doors had opened. "Now that Perth and Stirlingshire have seen fit to join us"—an extremely short woman wearing a camo jacket rolled her eyes, and a young guy barely out of his teens called out, "Sorry, Henry!"—"we can get started.

"It is the honor of the South Kingsferry Youth Twitching Club to host this year's Youth Big Day competition here on the grounds of Spence Castle. Thank you to a former member of my club, Calliope, and her parents, the new American residents here."

Dad shot Callie a quizzical look, which she pretended not to see.

"You have from the moment I blow my whistle until ten p.m. to record the species you find anywhere on the grounds, which encompass a bountiful one thousand acres. The boundaries are marked by the Marchbank Road to the north, the B800 to the east, Milton Farm to the south, and the Stewarton Polo Club to the west. Each team must stay together at all times. Your leaders will remain here at the castle, available via our phones should you require assistance, but we want to encourage our young birders to work together and make your identifications without our help.

"Take only pictures, leave only footprints. Keep your phones on silent. No recorded birdcalls, please. Do not approach any nesting birds." Mr. Hunt glared around at the assembled birders as though they'd already broken all these rules. "Any questions?"

Callie's dad raised his hand. She was struck by the sudden dread that he might ask Mr. Hunt then and there what he meant when he'd said Callie was a former member of his club. But instead, he jogged over to the steps and joined Mr. Hunt.

"Hello!" he called to the gathered birders. "I'm Pete Feldmeth. Welcome. So glad you all are here. Only thing I want to mention about the grounds—you're welcome to go anywhere, as Henry said. With one exception. Please don't go up in the castle keep. It's under renovation, and while

I imagine it would give you a pretty spectacular view, I'm afraid it's simply not safe."

"Understood?" Mr. Hunt waited until a mumble of agreement passed over the gathered youth twitchers. Many of them were obviously not completely awake yet.

"All right, then? Ready?"

Callie and Sid looked to each other with wide eyes. They had rescued a kitten from the secret passageways of an ancient castle. They had opened up to each other enough to become partners. They could do this.

"Set?"

"Good luck," Raj said to both of them, and only then did Callie realize that Raj would be birding with the absolute roasters instead of her.

"And . . . twitch!" Mr. Hunt let out a short blast on his whistle.

"Thanks. You too!"

The roaster named Silas grabbed Raj's arm and yanked him toward their group. "Have fun finding girl birds," Silas sneered at Callie as they went their way.

"We will!" Sid shouted at him. "You're right. What an absolute lavvy heid."

12 October 1939

Inverness

Mother cannot be bothered to write, but today
I got a letter from Father. Is it horrible that
I scanned it looking only for news of Charlie?
But once I saw there was none, I read again
for Father's news, which wasn't especially
interesting. He visited Mother at Spence, the
dogs are doing well, Mother misses me, blah
blah blah. He wrote to me on the train back to
London, trying to keep his business afloat with
so many of his employees off to war.

    I'm ashamed to say it took me a while to
notice, but when Mrs Miller hands out the post,
Magda's never gotten a letter. Though Mother
hasn't deigned to write to me, Father has
written, and my auntie Rebecca, and even our
housekeeper, Helen. June and Bea and Rosie all get
letters about as often as I do.

    While we devour our news from home, Magda
always prattles on about who even knows what,
telling jokes and being a nuisance and acting
like she hasn't a care in the world, which is
probably why it took me so long to realise she
wasn't getting word from home at all.

Until today, when she did.

She snatched that letter out of Mrs Miller's hand so quickly the poor lady gasped, and Magda went running out the front door. I waited for faithful June to go running after her mistress, or even Bea or Rosie. But no one did.

I slipped outside. I can't honestly say I was going to offer Magda whatever support she needed. Probably I was being nosy.

I found Magda under my favourite climbing tree, sobbing. I tried to back away, because I knew she wouldn't want to be seen like that, but I stepped on a twig and she was up in a flash.

"Come to enjoy my misery?" she snapped.

"I didn't know you'd be here." I turned to go, but she kept on.

"How was your letter?" she asked, her voice hard. "Did you even read it? I suppose when you get so many, they don't mean much."

"They mean everything," I said, and my voice caught. Because they do, even though they don't tell me anything real and they're no substitute for being back at home or knowing what's truly happening to my brother.

Then it was like all the fight went out of Magda and she slumped back under the tree, sniffling and refusing to say another word.

As she sat there, a nuthatch worked its way down the trunk above her head.

Curious birds, nuthatches. They're quite small, and aggressive, too. Unlike woodpeckers, who move up a trunk, nuthatches move down. On a journey from top to bottom, they spot insects that other birds won't see going up.

That's when I realised—maybe I'd been looking at Magda from the wrong angle.

CHAPTER NINETEEN

Instead of heading toward the forest or the pond like the other groups, Callie and Sid walked around to the far side of the castle. They knew a pair of extremely shy turtle-doves could be found feeding near a copse of trees toward the northern border of the property, but if the birds were scared off, they wouldn't show themselves for the rest of the day. If Callie and Sid found them first, they were likely to get at least one species none of the other groups would get.

The long walk paid off; Callie happily marked the European turtle-doves as their first sighting of the day, and it was quickly followed by sightings of bitterns, egrets, and gray plovers.

By the afternoon, though, Callie's feet ached. They hadn't spotted a new species for ages, and though Sid swore she'd heard the call of a corncrake, they could not find the bird anywhere they looked.

They did find an intriguing stone enclosure that looked for all the world like the outside of Mary Lennox's secret garden, but like that garden, they couldn't find a way inside.

"We're wasting time here," Callie complained as Sid poked and prodded at the stones.

"But there could be cool birds inside," Sid pointed out. "Imagine what a secure nesting spot it would be."

"Yeah, because there's no way in!"

The corncrake let out another loud, grating call. It definitely didn't sound like it was coming from inside the stone-walled garden.

"These competitions are dumb," Sid said.

"We'll find it," Callie insisted, sitting down to read the field guide's description of the corncrake for a fourth time, hoping to find some detail to help locate it.

"Maybe," Sid said. "But isn't it more fun to find birds without the pressure? This way, as soon as you find the bird, you're going to check it off a list and move on to the next one. You're not going to take the time to watch it or listen to it or appreciate how funny it looks when it runs with its body all flattened out."

"Wait, did you already see it? Today? Male or female?"

Sid shrugged. "I might have seen a female."

"Why didn't you say so?" Callie snapped the field guide shut and got to her feet, rolling out her neck, which ached from scanning the trees. "I get what you're saying. But can we be philosophical about bird-watching another day? I want to prove Mr. Hunt wrong! Are you helping me or not?"

Sid didn't respond. Callie's anger began to boil. "Sid?"

When she still didn't respond, Callie sighed and squatted to fit the field guide back in her backpack. It felt like the silent treatment, but it wasn't. This was an absence seizure. Not the kind where Sid would fall and hurt herself, but the kind where her brain misfired and she kind of went away for a minute. She was absent, even though she was right there.

Callie took a breath. Sid was right, when she thought about it. Going off on a quest to find birds because it was a passion and an interest, as it clearly had been for Pippa, was one thing. But doing it so she could prove something to someone who didn't care about her wasn't any different from going to a beach bonfire full of high schoolers only to prove something to people who were supposed to be her friends but clearly weren't.

CHAPTER TWENTY

"Come on, Callie," Lyla urged. "It's not that big a deal!"

It was a huge deal. They had snuck out of Imogen's house past the time when Callie was usually in bed. It hadn't been hard—Imogen's mom, Carole, was already enclosed in her own bedroom. But Callie had felt sick by the time they reached the end of the driveway.

It had always been extremely cool and convenient that her best friend lived a block away from the beach. When they were younger, it had been the best. Carole would take Callie and Imogen, set them up with towels and an umbrella, and hand them a wad of cash for the ice-cream cart. Then she'd pass out sunbathing while they played all day.

In the last year, it had changed. Imogen didn't want to go into the water anymore—it would mess up her hair. She didn't want to throw Frisbees or bury each other in the sand anymore—*We're not six years old.* All she wanted to do was "lay out" to work on her tan in her new two-piece, or walk down to the water's edge to flirt with the surfers.

To make matters worse, Lyla and Kate wanted to do the same things Imogen did. It didn't matter that Callie had been Imogen's best friend since the time in first grade when Imogen told off a group of boys who were taunting Callie on the playground. Now that Callie and Imogen wanted different things, Imogen only shrugged and did those things with Lyla and Kate instead. Callie had two choices: keep up or be left out.

Now, standing on a dark street late at night when her parents thought she was inside Imogen's house having a slumber party, those were still Callie's only choices.

"Go back inside if you want," Imogen said, turning toward the promise of high schoolers celebrating the end of the school year, the hope that some eyeliner and off-the-shoulder tops would convince them these barely middle-schoolers were worth talking to.

Lyla and Kate followed Imogen as she took off toward the beach. Callie tugged on the sparkly top Imogen had snuck out of her mom's closet and tried to ignore the plasticky feel of the lipstick coating her mouth.

"Wait up, you guys!"

The second her foot hit sand, she knew she'd made a mistake.

Callie had grown up on this beach. Not only all the time with Imogen and Carole. Callie and her family walked on the beach every Thanksgiving and Christmas, calling their families in the Midwest to gloat about the weather. Whenever anyone came from out of town, the beach was the first place they wanted to go. She'd even been there at night before, for a church s'mores party.

This was different.

The salty air was filled with laughter, but it was raucous, jarring laughter punctuated with swear words and insults. The smoke from the enormous bonfire mingled with cigarette and vape smoke, and empty beer cans littered the sand. The girls—the real high school girls—were beautiful and confident, like models, in their effortless makeup and easy fashion.

They hadn't spent hours getting ready. They didn't have to fake their glamour and maturity. Or maybe they did. But they were still worlds away from Callie and her friends, just graduated from sixth grade, standing on the edge of a cliff.

And the boys . . . the boys were men. At least to Callie. These were boys who shaved and drove cars and wouldn't give sixth graders a second glance, even if they were almost seventh graders.

Even Imogen looked daunted.

"We could go back," Callie said quietly, so Lyla and Kate wouldn't hear. "We could still say we were here."

That was all Imogen really wanted, Callie was pretty sure. To be able to say they'd gone to a high school bonfire.

Imogen threw back her shoulders and shook out her hair; some of it whapped Callie in the face. "Come on," she said, and headed straight for the cooler of drinks.

Callie tripped along behind the others, wishing she were invisible. She didn't want to throw herself into the midst of this any more than she wanted to stand there alone. But one option seemed distinctly worse than the other.

The cooler was guarded by a boy wearing only swim trunks, despite the bite in the air. He had an obvious surfer look about him—super tan and shaggy sun-kissed hair and a nose that was probably permanently burnt. "What's up, *chicas*?" he said, eyeing them. "You lost?"

"No," Imogen said, her voice haughty. Only Callie would notice the slight tremble. "We're thirsty."

He hooted. "Sassy—I like it!" He pulled back the lid on the cooler. "Just sodas," he said, "or I'm going to need to see some ID."

Imogen pouted and took a Diet Coke. "You're no fun," she said.

But Callie knew Imogen thought beer was disgusting. Her mom had offered them both a sip only a few months ago. Callie had declined. Imogen had spit hers out and ruined a whole pizza.

Lyla and Kate both grabbed sodas, and the guy turned to Callie. "How about you, sweetheart?"

Callie shook her head and stumbled back, tripping on the uneven sand.

"Don't mind her," Imogen said, rolling her eyes and sitting down on the cooler the guy had just shut. "Where do you go to school?"

"Yo, Fischer!" another guy yelled from a distance, hurling a Frisbee that caught the drink guy in the chest. "Who're your little friends?"

Fischer jumped to his feet. "Dude, you are going down!" He took off across the sand without a backward glance.

Imogen sighed. "He was sooo cute."

Lyla and Kate perched on either side of the cooler. There wasn't any room for Callie.

"You guys," she said. "Don't you think we should go back? We don't know anyone here."

"That's the whole point," Kate said. "These aren't stupid middle school boys."

Callie watched the Drink Guy tackle the Frisbee Guy. They were stupid high school boys.

"You can go back if you want," Imogen said. "I'm going to talk to those guys." She set her sights on a trio of boys in Torrey Pines baseball T-shirts near the fire, and Kate followed after Imogen.

Lyla hesitated.

"Want to go back with me?" Callie said.

Lyla twisted her hair around her finger. "And do what? Sit at the door waiting for Imogen to get back with her key? Otherwise we have to wake Carole up, and she'll find out we snuck out."

"We could ask Imogen for her key," Callie said.

Lyla shook her head and stood up. "No, thanks. Imogen would never let us forget it." She pulled a tube of lip gloss from her pocket and applied another coat to her already glossy lips. "Anyway, it's not that big a deal. It's only a party."

And then Callie was alone with the cooler. Full of beer. The bubble-gum-sweet smell of vape smoke curled its way around her, and she knew that when her mom washed these clothes, she'd just think the smell had come from lotion or shampoo or something.

It was scary how easy this had all been.

She sat on the cooler, wishing she had a phone to look busy with. But that was yet another thing she was behind on. She didn't even really want one, except for situations like this. Imogen had gotten one when she turned ten, and they'd had fun with selfies and filters and games before Imogen had gotten private about her phone.

A group of girls appeared in front of Callie, talking and laughing.

"Um," one of them said. "Can you move?"

Callie stood so they could open the cooler. She felt totally stupid standing there like the drink monitor, but she didn't know what else to do.

"Hey, are you okay?" a girl with waist-length blond hair said.

Callie nodded, but her eyes brimmed with tears.

"You look kind of young. Are you someone's kid sister?"

She shook her head again. They were going to think she was mute.

The rest of the girls moved on with their drinks, but the blond girl stayed. "Are you here with someone?"

The obvious answer was that she was here with Imogen and Lyla and Kate. But was that true if they were over there, trying to talk to high school boys, and wouldn't even notice if she left?

"My friends are over there," she finally said.

The girl looked across the fire at Callie's friends, so painfully young compared to the high school boys they'd attached themselves to. But the boys were talking to them anyway. Callie's stomach turned. "Well, that's not good," the girl said. "I'm guessing you're the sensible one who knew this was a bad idea?"

"Sensible," Callie said. "Or scared."

"Same difference." The girl pulled her hair into a top-knot so fast Callie would have missed it if she'd blinked. "Being afraid doesn't have to be a bad thing. Keeps you out of situations you're not ready for. But right now? It really sucks."

It did suck. Callie stared at her friends, willing even one of them to look over her way. Maybe they'd be impressed she was talking to this high school girl. But mostly she wanted to know they still remembered she existed.

"You know what else? Your friends are scared too. And if they're not, they're really dumb." The girl pulled out her phone. "Do you want to call someone? To come pick you up?"

If Imogen would never let them forget asking for her house key, Callie would definitely never live down calling her mommy to get picked up. But as she watched, one of the baseball boys handed his can of beer to Lyla, and she took it. And she drank.

"Yeah, thanks," Callie said.

The girl walked Callie out to the street and waited with her until her mom pulled up. "I'll watch out for your friends," she promised.

"Thanks." Callie walked on wobbly legs to the car, avoiding her mom's worried gaze.

"You're the brave one," the girl called after her. "You know that, right?"

Callie didn't feel like the brave one when her parents lectured her about peer pressure and making good choices. (Which she had! Eventually, anyway!) She didn't feel brave begging her mother not to call Imogen's mom. She swore over and over to Imogen that she hadn't meant for the other parents to find out, but sometimes, deep down, she wondered if she had wanted that to happen. She had hoped that someone could step in and make Imogen stop, bring back the Imogen of sandcastles and bunny-eared selfies.

But what happened instead was Imogen's mom called Lyla's and Kate's parents, and everyone got in trouble. Kate's parents even called the high school to rat out the baseball players, so some high schoolers got in trouble for giving alcohol to younger kids. (And having alcohol in the first place.)

The absolute worst part was when Imogen showed up at Callie's door with Lyla and Kate in tow and Callie thought, for the tiniest second, that maybe her oldest friend was going to apologize for getting them all into the whole mess, and Callie would have forgiven her too, not only for that, but for the whole last year of distance and secrets and eye rolls.

Instead Imogen shoved a box at Callie, told her she hated her and couldn't believe she'd ever been friends with her, she'd only been taking pity on her, but she was done with that and Callie better not speak to her ever again.

Callie didn't cry. Not right away. She watched in shock as the three girls turned as one and marched off.

Imogen lost her temper sometimes. She said nasty things. But she'd never said she hated Callie.

Callie sank onto the floor right there next to the front door and opened the box. There was the stuffed octopus she'd given Imogen in third grade, slashed to pieces. Also slashed—the tie-dyed shirt they'd made together and passed back and forth until it didn't fit them anymore. A strip of photos from one of those booths, with Callie's face x-ed out in every one. The copy of *Matilda* Callie had given Imogen in fourth grade, a chunk of pages savagely ripped out.

The only undamaged thing in the box was Imogen's half of the heart necklace they shared; Callie's half was hanging on a chain around her neck that very moment.

Sitting there with a broken heart in her hand, Callie finally began to cry.

15 October 1939
Inverness

Magda's kept to herself for several days, and the other girls seem lost. I've taken them on some birding walks, pointing out birds they'd never noticed before.

Bushtits, which remind me of Rosie. They're smaller than hummingbirds and don't look like they could be of any use at all, but any gardener would tell you they're aces at getting rid of pests in a garden.

Willow warblers, who are a shade of greenish brown exactly like Bea's eyes, and they moult their feathers fully twice a year, rather like Bea leaving a trail of her things everywhere she goes throughout the house.

We didn't spot a common poorwill, since they only live in North America. But I told June about what I've read of them—the rare bird that hibernates through cold weather, lowering its heartbeat and breathing and body temperature for weeks at a time. I told June that was her bird because of how she sleeps like a hibernating animal, but also because of how well she's adapted to her new surroundings.

We didn't see a Kestrel, either, but if we had, I would have thought of Magda. I don't know that I'd have told her that, but if anyone's a small, fierce hunter, it's Magda.

CHAPTER TWENTY-ONE

Sid and Callie paused outside the keep, Sid retying her shoelaces and Callie grabbing a swig of water. They needed to regroup, figure out what they might find as the late afternoon fell, and map out where they needed to be and when, in order to spot those species.

Sid was right. Proving themselves to Mr. Hunt would feel good. But being here with Sid, knowing they had each other's backs, that was way better motivation.

Sid pulled out the list they'd made over the last week. Callie pulled out Pippa's journal. "I was really hoping you could see a hoopoe," Sid said. "I swear I saw one the first week we moved in."

"Oh, me too," Callie said, thinking of Pippa's drawing of a crazy zebra-striped bird with a headdress of feathers sticking straight up. "We might smell it before we see it."

"Huh?"

"The babies and females give off a terrible odor to scare away predators," Callie said.

Sid looked to Callie with eyebrows raised. "Wow. I didn't know that."

Callie grinned. "I know a thing or two."

"Never said you didn't."

"Well even if we don't see it today, we'll go looking for it another time."

They both quieted when they heard voices and laughter. But no other groups were visible on the rolling hills beyond the castle. Then, from inside the wall they were leaning on, five boys tumbled out, laughing and hushing one another.

Mr. Hunt's club went silent when they saw Callie and Sid outside the forbidden keep. Raj's face was ashen.

Callie jammed Pippa's journal into her bag. "You went into the keep?"

There was no point lying. Even if they could have gotten away with it, Callie had a feeling Silas was proud of breaking the only rule her father had laid out. He probably didn't think the American non-noble had any right to make rules about the Scottish castle. He shrugged. "So?"

"So it's totally unsafe! You could have been killed!"

"Aww, afraid you'd miss me too much?"

Sid pulled her phone from her pocket. "I won't miss you in this competition," she said. "Pretty sure this'll disqualify you."

"Wait—"

Silas looked around wildly, like there was anything he could offer them. The other boys all looked to Silas, and Callie was suddenly struck by all the pressure Imogen must have felt, with Lyla and Kate and even Callie always assuming she'd have the answers.

Not that she felt any pity for Silas. But maybe for Imogen. Maybe a little.

Raj stood apart, staring at the ground.

"Go ahead," Callie said to Sid. She'd make the call herself if she had her own phone. "They can explain themselves to Mr. Hunt."

"No, look," Silas said. "We got so many good birds from the view up there. We got an osprey!"

"By cheating."

"Yeah. No. Look, just . . . if you don't say anything, you can go up and spot those birds too. We won't tell anyone else."

"How is that your offer?" Sid spluttered. "'If you don't tell that we cheated, you can cheat too!'"

"Your loss." Silas's moment of panic had passed. "If it's

your word against ours, who do you think Mr. Hunt's going to believe?"

The skinny one held up his hand, and Silas high-fived it. The other boys hooted. Except Raj. He looked miserable. He looked like he'd been dragged up into the keep by boys he should have stood up to, but hadn't been able to. Standing up was hard, even when you knew right from wrong, especially when you knew your status was already shaky and belonging felt more important than moral victory.

Callie could have stayed at Imogen's house that night. She'd been pressured to go to the beach, but no one had forced her. She'd made a mistake. And once she had, there was no way out. But maybe Raj deserved a way out.

"Come on, lads." Silas gave a low bow and tipped his dorky hat like some sort of gentleman. "Lassies."

They took off toward the forest. Raj stayed planted. "I'm really sorry," he said. "It was so stupid."

"Yeah," Callie agreed.

"Frodo!" Silas called. "Come on! The group has to stay together!"

"Cares about rules now, does he?" Sid muttered.

"Look," Callie said, before she could think better of it. "You don't have to go with those bampots."

Raj cracked a smile.

"You can come with us."

"I can?" Raj said at the same time that Sid said, "He can?"

"We're already rogue birders," Callie said, shrugging. "What's one more rule-breaker?"

Raj looked at Sid. "Is it okay with you?"

She held out her fist. "Team Rogue Birders, I guess."

Raj bumped her fist, then turned to the retreating backs of Mr. Hunt's club. "Oi, Silas!" he shouted. "You've never even read Lord of the Rings! Frodo is a hero!"

18 October 1939
Inverness

A group of ravens is called an unkindness. Guess who told me that? Magda. More specifically, she called ME a raven, and said I belong with an unkindness of my own kind.

She'd heard about my bird walks with the other girls, and how I assigned them bird familiars.

She's not wrong, not really. I've been terrible and standoffish with her and the other girls too. I've snapped and acted haughty. I was scared and anxious and homesick, but so's she. We all are. She copes by being an insufferable know-it-all. Apparently I cope by being completely beastly.

But you know what I told Magda? Ravens are supersmart. They can adapt to live anywhere — among people in cities, or deep in the wilderness. They recognize human faces and they hold funerals for one another and their problem-solving skills are even better than gorillas'.

I told Magda that maybe I am a raven. But I think she might be too.

For a moment, I thought she was going to punch me. She probably thought better of it, because I would have screamed and then we both would have ended up cleaning out the chicken coop again.

Instead she said, "I can't be a raven, because I haven't got a flock."

"But you have," I said. "You've only been separated. The war will end eventually and you'll return to your family."

"I won't," she said. "Father died in the mines last year, and Mother died of influenza right before the war broke out. All I have in the world are my brothers James and Henry and Matthew, and they are all, every one of them, headed to the front lines."

If Magda's brothers don't make it home from the war, she'll have no one. Really and truly.

The letter she'd gotten had informed her of an injury her brother Henry had sustained in training. Apparently he's broken his leg in three places and is being tended in an army hospital.

It's horrible. And maybe this wasn't the right thing to say. But it's what came out: "But Magda," I told her, "at least that means they can't send him into battle."

And for a bright, shining moment, I saw a flicker of hope in her eyes.

CHAPTER TWENTY-TWO

Silas was right. Mr. Hunt was not going to believe Callie and Sid if they reported the boys for going into the keep.

But that was the only thing he was right about.

The playing field wasn't level; it wasn't fair, but it was how things were. Mya-Rose Craig wrote that girl birders had to be five times better than boys to get the same respect. But she didn't let that stop her. She made it her goal to *be* five times better, because that was what it took.

Callie, Sid, and Raj were better birders than Silas and those bampots, simply because they actually cared about the birds. They would do their best. Maybe that meant they'd win, at least on their terms. Maybe they wouldn't.

But no matter where they placed, they'd know they'd done it honestly.

They agreed that combining their lists wouldn't be fair; they'd proceed with Callie and Sid's list so far. But there was no point in wasting Raj's knowledge. He quickly helped them add three more species his group had already found.

They were camped next to the starling tree, waiting for the flock to return for the evening, when Sid's phone rang.

She frowned. "That's not Pops's number."

Callie peered at the screen. "I think it's my mom's."

"Hello?" Sid said.

Callie and Raj watched as Sid dropped the guidebook, her face awash with horror.

"We're—" Her brows furrowed as she looked around wildly; then she shoved the phone at Callie. "Tell her where we are."

"Mom?" Callie said. "We're on the far side of the pond, by that giant oak. What's—"

"Okay, we're coming to get you," Mom said, and then hung up.

Sid stood frozen, gaze unfocused, staring into space like she was having a seizure, except her eyes weren't blank. They were terrified. Raj hovered nearby, unsure what to do.

"Sid?" Callie said.

"It's Pops," was all Sid could manage to say.

* * *

A couple of minutes later, the tiny car appeared, bouncing along the dirt path not meant for motor vehicles. Callie's mom was at the wheel, Dad in the passenger seat, and Jax in back.

"Mom, what's going on?" Callie asked as Sid dove inside the car, hardly waiting for it to stop.

"Ben had a heart attack," Mom said. "We're taking Sid to the hospital. You can stay and finish the competition, if you want."

There wasn't any question where Callie needed to be at this moment. Part of being five times better also meant understanding when adding birds to a list was the least important thing.

"No, I'm coming," Callie said. She turned helplessly to Raj. "I'm sorry. I pulled you away from your group and now—"

"Don't be a roaster," he said, pushing her toward the car.

"Can you get back all right, hon?" Callie's mom asked Raj. "I'm afraid there's no more room in the car."

Callie was barely squeezing the door shut; they definitely couldn't fit Raj in.

"I'm fine, ma'am," Raj said. "Callie, do you want me to take your forms? I can turn them in for you. Just . . . so you get credit for your work."

It hardly mattered now. And a tiny part of Callie wondered what Raj might do with those forms. He could join back up with Silas's group and give them Callie and Sid's sightings.

"We've got to go," Dad said from the front seat.

But if there was a chance she could show those boys and Mr. Hunt what she'd done—what *they'd* done—even with the odds stacked against them . . . Callie shoved the forms out the window at Raj. "Thank you," she said. "I'm sorry!"

The hospital waiting room smelled like bleach and despair. But anything was better than being packed into the tiny car next to a rigid Sid, barely breathing except for the occasional shuddery sob.

Callie wanted to tell her it would be okay. But maybe it wouldn't. Maybe Ben would die. What would Sid do then? Where would she go?

Jax started bouncing off the walls the moment they stepped foot in the hospital, fueled by adrenaline and what probably felt like a grand adventure to him. Dad hustled him off to find a cafeteria or vending machine, in order to get his exuberant energy away from Sid.

"Hello," Mom said to the nurse at the front desk. "Can you give me information on Ben MacDonald's condition?"

At first the nurses wouldn't tell Mom anything about

Ben's condition, because she wasn't family. But they wouldn't tell Sid anything because she was a minor.

"Honey," Mom said to Sid. "I don't want to embarrass you, but I'm about to go full American, okay?"

Sid didn't say anything. At this point Callie couldn't even tell if she was seizing or functioning on some kind of autopilot state.

"Do it, Mom," Callie said. She didn't care how embarrassing her mom acted if they could find out what was going on with Ben.

"I'm sorry," Mom said, raising her voice, "but that man in there is this young lady's sole guardian. What's more, she's *his* only family. And I am his employer. I was led to believe the United Kingdom health care system was superior to the American one, but I'm starting to have my doubts! Do you mean to withhold his information forever, since he has no adult family members? Honestly!"

Under normal circumstances, Callie would have been crawling under one of the hard plastic waiting room seats. But now she slipped her hand into her mom's and gave a squeeze.

The nurse sighed, threw a glance heavenward, then said, "One moment, please."

Ben had been driving back from his interview, the doctor told Callie's mom, and drove into a ditch when the heart attack came on. A passerby called for an ambulance, and then called Callie's parents, because their number was listed on the landscaping plans in Ben's truck. They'd hoped someone would know how to get in touch with Ben's family.

"We're his family," Mom said firmly.

When he reached the hospital, doctors stabilized him, but then there were complications and he'd been rushed into surgery. He'd only just gotten out and was being closely monitored in intensive care. They wouldn't be able to see him until he was more stable. Not until the morning, definitely.

"Are you sure there's not any . . . other family?" the doctor asked, glancing over at Sid, who suddenly looked incredibly young and small and alone.

"It's only us," Mom said quietly.

He frowned and made a note on the chart. "We'll keep you informed," he said, then bustled away.

Jax and Dad returned with armfuls of vending-machine bounty, none of it familiar to Callie, but she took something vaguely chocolate-and-nut-shaped. Jax climbed into the chair next to Sid and leaned his head on her shoulder.

"Don't bother her, Jax," Callie said.

But Sid leaned into Jax. "He's fine."

They sat together, quiet except for the ticking clock and the distant buzzes and beeps from rooms down the hall. Callie wanted to say something or do something that could make the situation better. But there was nothing to do but be there with Sid, and wait.

When Jax let out a huge yawn, Dad said, "If we're not going to know more until the morning, should we consider going back home? You'd stay with us, of course, Sid," he added.

"I'm not leaving," she said. "You guys can go. I'll be fine."

"Why don't you take Jax and Callie back?" Mom said to Dad. "I'll stay with Sid and keep you guys posted."

"I'm staying," Callie said. "I mean, I want to. Please? Can I?"

"All right," Mom said. She drew Jax into a hug. "Go with Dad, okay? Get some rest and feed Mr. Collywobbles, and come back tomorrow, okay, bud?"

He nodded, the adrenaline worn off and the sugar crash impending.

Dad gave Callie a quick hug and put a hand on Sid's shoulder. "Hang in there," he said.

When the nurse realized they were staying, she showed them to a more private room for families who were waiting on intensive care patients. There were couches and blankets and a coffee maker. The lights were low, unlike the harsh fluorescent light from before.

But it was still a hospital waiting room, where people

waited to hear horrible, life-changing news. The endless beeps and buzzes continued, and the drone of the PA system telling doctors where they were needed. Nothing as dramatic as the code blues on television, but made somehow worse by being so relentless.

An elderly woman sat stock-still in one corner of the room, and Callie was struck by the urge to see if she was breathing.

Sid took a blanket and curled up alone in an armchair. Callie and her mom curled together on a couch, and soon Mom was lightly snoring. Callie tried to rest. She wanted to have energy if Sid needed her. But there was no way she could sleep.

She carefully hauled her backpack onto the couch, trying not to jostle her mom. Pippa's journal was soft in Callie's hands, softer than the hospital blanket over her lap. She opened it up and read through the list of birds in the first part of the journal. She'd given Raj their competition logs, but she thought she remembered which ones on Pippa's list she and Sid had spotted before the phone call.

Some of Pippa's more unique birds had been spotted in other parts of the country, and even on trips to other parts of Europe. But Callie read over the entries of birds spotted on the castle grounds that she hadn't yet seen. Were they still there? Or were they a species that had moved on, or worse, gone extinct? It didn't seem like much had changed on the castle grounds in the last eighty years, but the world around it had changed a lot. Her parents had even commented on how much South Kingsferry had changed since they'd lived there twenty years earlier.

And yet so many of the birds were the same. So much about Pippa's life, as different as it had been, was just like Callie's.

Callie flipped farther back in the journal to where Pippa had done drawings and written more notes about the birds.

There was a raven, sharp-eyed, calculating. Pippa had captured the fearsome beak perfectly. Imogen was a raven. But the thing about ravens was, as intimidating as they could be, stuff of nightmares and dark fairy tales, they were incredibly smart. They observed everything in their surroundings, they remembered, and they survived.

There was a starling, always in formation with a flock of its own kind. Lyla hadn't wanted to go to the bonfire either. She hadn't wanted to talk to high school boys or drink beer. She probably hadn't even wanted to blacklist Callie from their group and spread lies about her to the whole school. But her fear of being cast out of Imogen's flock was even stronger than the rest of her fears.

There was a nuthatch, small, aggressive, working its way down a tree trunk rather than up. Who cared it if looked silly? It would find the juiciest insects. When Callie had first met Sid, she never would have dreamed they'd end up here together. Their first impressions of each other had been terrible. They kept working their way down the trunk.

When Callie finally drifted off to sleep, Pippa's journal was spread open on her lap, and the raven's eye was trained on her. Calculating, maybe. Or maybe also watching over her.

20 October 1939

Inverness

I finally got a letter from Mother. Three letters, actually. She'd written them ages ago, but the post had gotten diverted for some reason. She chided me for the trouble I'd caused with the chickens, but also applauded my ingenuity. She said my night in the chicken coop sounded awful, but that nothing would be more awful than if I came to harm because she couldn't bear to send me away.

In her other letters, written before the chicken incident, she mostly complained about how dull her life was without all her society functions, or how lonely the house felt with everyone gone, or how Anne and Diana woke her too early in the morning, insisting on going outside.

My heart squeezed at the thought of Anne and Diana pining away for me, the only one who understands their needs. I'll admit I wanted to lash out at Mother for complaining about my precious girls, when I would give anything to be with them again.

But Magda's situation has made me look at my

own with a more generous eye. The main thing
is to hope her brothers return from the war, but
if they sustain any injuries, they'll be no use in
the mines. If her family is to survive, at least
one of her brothers must return able-bodied.

I've been such a horrid beast, angry at
Mother for trying to protect me. If the worst
should happen to Charlie, or even Father, at least
Mother and I would have each other. And Anne and
Diana.

So instead I wrote to Mother and explained
that Anne and Diana love to sleep in, if only she
would take them for a walk right before turning
in at night, which will also help her sleep as
well. And then, if she lets them sleep in the
bedroom with her—preferably on the bed, and
why wouldn't she want that comfort, alone in the
castle as she is—they will happily sleep until
noon.

And then we shall all sleep more easily.

CHAPTER TWENTY-THREE

Callie woke with a start when her mother stood up.

"Oh, wow, how good of you to come," Mom said to someone, but Callie's eyes were sleep-encrusted, and the morning light from the windows was blinding. She turned her face into the pillow.

"I'm Jennifer," she said. "Callie's mom."

"Vik," she heard a deep voice say. "Rajesh's dad."

Callie jerked her head up. There stood Raj and a stout, dark-haired man in a sweater-vest and glasses.

"My wife couldn't get off work," the man said. "But she sent you this." He held out some Tupperware containers and set them on the coffee table.

"That's so lovely," Mom said. "Callie? You awake? Your friend is here."

Callie sat all the way up. "Hi," she said to Raj. Then her brain finally caught up to the situation, and her eyes flew to the chair where Sid had fallen asleep the night before. "Where's Sid?"

Mom blinked at the chair. Judging by her smooshed hair and the weird wrinkle on the side of her face, she hadn't been awake long. "Bathroom, maybe?"

"Can I make you some coffee?" Raj's dad asked, busying himself over by the window with the ancient machine.

"That would be lovely," Mom said. "I'm going to check the bathroom," she told Callie, leaving her with Raj.

"You didn't have to come," Callie said, then wondered if that was rude. It wasn't that she was ungrateful—just surprised. Shocked, really. Back home, if there'd been a family emergency, the only person she could have imagined might show up at a hospital waiting room was Grandma Feldmeth. But Raj and his dad stood there like it was totally normal.

"Yeah, we did," Raj said. "Mum said you'd be hungry. She's convinced her rasam rice makes everything better."

Callie's stomach growled. "It might."

Raj started opening the Tupperware containers and explaining what was in each of his mother's Indian dishes. Callie served herself some sweet upma, a raisin-studded porridge. It might have been the fact that she hadn't eaten since her bag lunch halfway through the Big Day, but in that moment, the creamy porridge was the most delicious thing she had ever eaten in her entire life.

"Did your team win?" she asked Raj.

He looked at her blankly.

"The Big Day."

"You guys were my team," he said. "We did great. Even Mr. Hunt was impressed."

"But Silas and them won?"

"They would have," Raj said. "If I hadn't told the group leaders what happened. Silas was right that Mr. Hunt wouldn't believe you. But I thought there was a chance he'd believe me. Which is totally not right, but I figured I might as well try."

Raj had stood up to his friends, not only in defecting from their group, but in an even bigger way. That was more startling than the fact that he sat across from her in a hospital waiting room while they waited for news about her best friend's grandfather.

Her best friend.

"And did he? Believe you?"

Raj hesitated. "He didn't want to. But I told all four of the adult leaders together. They had a whole argie-bargie about it." He grinned at the look on her face. "Argument. In the end, the team was disqualified. Title went to Perth. You should have seen Mr. Hunt's face."

It would have been so easy for Raj to crack a few jokes about *those doaty girls* and join back up with his buddies. The kids he'd known forever, whose approval he probably needed at school. But he hadn't. He'd turned in their forms and called himself part of their team and used his standing to do what was right.

Callie had been so disappointed in Raj outside the library, when he went off to play video games with boys who were clearly jerks. But that hadn't been the end of the story. Just like the night of the bonfire wasn't the end of Callie's story. And this right here, this awful night in the hospital and whatever news would come about Ben, wouldn't be the end of Sid's story. Callie wouldn't let it be.

Raj motioned toward Pippa's journal on the table. "What's that?"

"Oh." Raj had more than earned a glimpse into Pippa's journal. "You should take a look. I found it in the castle."

"Cal?" Mom said, reappearing with slightly less-smooshed hair. "Sid wasn't in the bathroom. Any idea where she might be?"

"She has a phone, right?" Raj said. "Could you call her?"

"Right."

As her mom dialed, Callie stood, her whole body stiff and weird from half sleeping on the hospital couch. The ring came from nearby—too nearby. Raj reached beneath the cushion of the chair where Sid had been sleeping and pulled out the ringing phone.

"I'm going to look for her." Callie didn't wait for her mom to protest or Raj to say he'd join her. She was so grateful he was there, but she needed to think.

The hospital was enormous. Sid could be anywhere. Or worse, she could have left the hospital and truly be anywhere. But, Callie reminded herself, she had to narrow her focus. If Sid were a bird, she'd go to the most likely habitat, the place that met her needs.

By Ben's side.

Heavy double doors blocked off the intensive care hallway. Doctors and nurses passed through only by flashing badges at a sensor on the wall. But Sid wouldn't have let a little thing like high security keep her from her pops.

Callie edged closer to the door.

A doctor gave her a funny look but passed through without saying anything.

In a movie, she'd find a way to steal one of those badges. But Callie had no heist skills, and besides, what if a stolen badge meant a doctor couldn't get to an ICU patient when they were needed?

When a nurse left the nearby nurses' station, Callie hurried over to the doors and peered through the windows. All she saw was yet another long, fluorescent-white hallway. Pale blue curtains were drawn across the doorways, and carts with computers dotted the hallway. No Sid in sight.

"Out of the way, please," barked a doctor in plain scrubs and a Wonder Woman cap.

Callie was considering trying her luck at following the doctor through the doors when Sid said, "Looking for me?"

She was puffy-faced, with dark bags beneath her eyes. She looked like she'd slept in a chair after her beloved grandfather had had a life-threatening heart attack.

"Sid!" Callie threw her arms around her friend, realizing the full force of how worried she'd been, how much Sid had come to mean to her, and also how they had never hugged before. "Are you okay? I mean, of course you're not okay. We tried to call you, but you left your phone."

Sid slumped down the side of the wall and sat right there, totally in the way of all the hustle and bustle around them. Callie ignored the glare from the nurse returning to her station and joined Sid on the floor.

"This is as close as they'll let me get," Sid said. She looked so small and alone.

"Is it okay if I sit here with you?"

Sid nodded.

They sat in silence for a long time. Or at least, not talking, but around them the hospital continued to buzz. Eventually Callie's mom came around the corner and saw them sitting there. Callie gave her a little wave to show they were okay, and Mom withdrew back to the waiting area.

"Your mum is so great," Sid said.

Callie waited. She wanted to know more about Sid's mom. About anything Sid wanted to tell her, really. But she was afraid that if she asked, Sid would withdraw again. She had let Callie sit with her. Even if she didn't say another word, that would be something.

But Sid didn't withdraw. "My mum had me when she was really young," she went on. "My dad was never in the picture, and my grandma died the year before I was born. Cancer. So my mum and I lived with Pops. She started university, but she was also working in a pub, trying to save money so we could get our own place. It was a lot of stress, I guess."

The ICU doors opened from the inside and a doctor ushered a couple through. The man was sobbing. The woman was pale. When they'd reached the elevator and gotten on, Sid continued.

"Mum started drinking. I guess she drank before I was born too, but she'd stopped as soon as she realized she was pregnant. It was bad this time. Especially because drinking causes seizures. And seizures made her feel out of control, which made her drink more."

"Ben said your mom had the same epilepsy you do."

"Aye. Of all the things she could have given me . . .

When I was four, Pops told her she couldn't stay with him anymore, if she didn't stop drinking. But he wouldn't let her take me either. I was tiny, but I swear I still remember them screaming at each other."

Callie couldn't imagine Ben screaming at anyone. Unless that person was putting Sid in danger. She laid her hand palm up on the floor between them. Sid laid hers down on top of Callie's and intertwined their fingers.

"She kinda disappeared. Hardly ever came around, and when she did, it was to beg Pops for money. Then a couple years later, car crash, she was gone. It's been just the two of us ever since. I guess it's always been the two of us, really."

Even when Callie had lost all her friends, she'd always had her mom and dad. Grandma Feldmeth. And she was for sure stuck with Jaxy for the rest of her life. But if Ben didn't make it, Sid would be truly alone. At least as far as family.

Family was important. Callie was so lucky to have hers. But it wasn't the only thing. She squeezed Sid's hand and held on tight.

When Callie and Sid returned to the private waiting area a few hours later, with numb backsides and growling stomachs, Callie thought at first that they had the wrong room. Several people she didn't know milled around, dipping into the Tupperwares on the table. But then Jax came running up to her and she realized Dad was back too. Raj and his father were still there, playing cards.

"Raj taught me War and I totally beat him!" Jax announced.

Raj looked up and grinned. "Quite the card shark, that one. Hullo, Sid. We're pulling for your pops."

"Thanks." Sid looked to Callie in wonder. Callie shrugged, as surprised as she was that Raj and his father had come.

"We all are," said another voice.

Callie turned in surprise. "Esme?"

The librarian stood there, as out of place as a teacher in a grocery store. "Pulling for Ben, I mean. How are you, girls? Are you huggers?"

Sid hung back, but Callie nodded and fell into Esme's warm hug.

"There's quite a lot to eat, if you're hungry," Esme said. "Raj's mum makes the best Indian food I've ever had. And I've been to India. I brought biscuits. They're just from a tin, but sugar's sugar."

"Thanks, Esme. Have you seen my mom?"

"Talking to the doctor." Esme nodded toward the corner of the room, where Callie's mom stood with a woman in scrubs.

Sid bolted over to listen in on the discussion, and Callie wavered on whether to follow.

"Maybe best give her space?" Esme suggested gently.

"Why are you here?" Callie blurted. "I mean, I'm glad, I just—how did you even know?"

"Oh, librarians," Esme said with a smile. "We make it our business to know things."

"Oh," Callie said. "Yeah."

"I'm joking you. Defense mechanism for serious situations." Esme shrugged sheepishly. "Truth is, I ran into Henry at the grocery this morning. Mr. Hunt? He told me what happened. And I . . . did you know I went to school with Sid's mum?"

"Sid's mum?"

"Aye, we were really good mates, actually. Until Third Year, when she started running with a rougher crowd. But I'd always liked her dad. And I just . . . When I heard he was here . . . Is it weird that I came?"

"No," Callie said. It *was* kind of weird that she had come. It was weird that Raj and his dad had come and that his mom had made food for them when she barely knew them. It was weird, but it was kind of wonderful.

Maybe, even when Callie had thought she was all alone, there had been people who would show up for her if she needed them. Now she was determined to be one of those people for Sid.

"Excuse me, everyone?" The room went silent as Callie's mom spoke up from the corner. Sid stood a little behind her, and Callie couldn't read her face. "I've just spoken with the doctor, and it looks like Ben's going to be all right."

Everyone cheered, including the people Callie didn't know.

"That's Angus from the hardware store," Esme murmured into Callie's ear when she saw her looking. "And Chester from the pub. Wallace over there, I think he played football with Ben back in the day."

"What about her?" Callie asked, nodding toward an older woman with a ton of makeup and piles of curls atop her head.

Esme rolled her eyes a little. "Chester's lady of the week."

"He won't be able to have visitors for a while yet," Mom went on, "and only family at first. So we really appreciate you all coming out. But please feel free to head home and we'll keep you posted on developments."

"Wait," Sid added, before anyone could leave. "Thank you. Just ... thank you all for coming. I didn't know Pops had ... people. Like you. Thank you."

"I'll be right back," Callie said to Esme, then rushed over to Sid.

This time Sid was the one who hugged Callie. "Thank you," she said, sniffling into Callie's shoulder.

"I didn't do anything," Callie said.

"Of course you did. You were here."

"That's what friends do." Callie pulled away and looked carefully at Sid. "You have people too, you know."

"What?"

"It's not only Ben. These people are here for you, too. And if anything had happened . . . but it didn't. I'm just saying. You have people."

Callie had people too, even beyond her family. If sometimes after this she fought with Sid or felt let down by Raj, it wouldn't mean sudden catastrophic solitude. If she got kicked out of another club or made another really dumb decision, there would still be ways to move forward. There would be people to turn to.

And just like those people would be there for Callie, she had to do the same for them. Ben might be on the mend this time, but he was getting too old for their nomadic lifestyle. He and Sid both needed more stability. A place to call home. Thankfully Callie knew of a cottage where two very special people might make a home and become a part of a larger family.

Sid wiped at her eyes. "Thank you."

"Thank you," Callie said. Sid probably didn't even know what Callie was thanking her for. It didn't matter. Callie knew.

24 October 1939

Inverness

I saw a murmuration of starlings today.

Murmuration is the collective noun for
starlings, like an unkindness of ravens, or a
parliament of owls, or a scold of jays. But with
starlings, it's also the name of this thing
they do all together at the end of a day, before
swooping into a nesting spot and tucking in,
safe for the night.

The moment I spotted them, I called for the
others. I called for Magda, specifically. I don't
know why, but I knew she needed to see them.
And she came. They all did, even Mrs Miller.

Starlings fly together, not in formation like
a flock of migrating gulls. No, starlings form
these massive groups—sometimes thousands of
birds in one murmuration—that aren't only flying.
They're dancing. And the mass of birds tumbles
together, up and down and around the sky.

"How do they do that?" Rosie marvelled.

Sometimes they form shapes, like clouds, and
just as permanent, because one moment they're a
whale and next a rose and next a dream.

It seems impossible, that they would be able

to work together, so very many of them. Because they're quiet, too. They're not calling out to turn this way or that.

Can they read one another's minds?

It turns out they don't have to keep track of every other starling in the murmuration. Each one only keeps track of the six or seven other birds around them. But that awareness spreads throughout the flock—the murmuration—and they dance like they were choreographed and rehearsed and this is the final performance of a storied career on the stage.

Only the next night, they'll do it all over again.

There are six of us here—Magda and June, Bea and Rosie, Mrs Miller and myself. If I let myself think of all the children evacuated from their homes, all the parents praying the children will return safely, all the soldiers on the front lines, I almost can't breathe. But I can manage to think of Magda and June, Bea and Rosie, Mrs Miller and myself.

And it's rather a nice thought to imagine each of them keeping track of me.

CHAPTER TWENTY-FOUR

Callie's parents considered moving Ben and Sid into the castle while he recovered, but everyone ultimately decided the cottage was easier to keep warm and cozy, and if Ben called out, Sid could always hear him from a room away. The castle was near enough for someone to be there in minutes if they needed something.

Not only Callie and her family, either.

Ben's friends from the pub and the hardware store and "back in the day" started coming around. He hadn't thought it proper to invite them to the grounds before, but Callie's dad had befriended them all at the hospital and made clear they were welcome. He'd need someone to test out the golf course as soon as it was ready, after all.

Esme came every few days with stacks of books for Ben, and when Sid found out Esme had known her mom, Esme began to tell endless stories of their childhood, of puppet shows and paper dolls and pranks. Of when Cate, Sid's mom, began to have her own absence seizures, and the time Esme punched a boy who called her slow.

"I was wondering," Esme said one afternoon when Ben had dozed off in his chair, "what do you two think about giving twitching another go?"

Callie wrinkled her nose, and Sid got up and started clearing the tea things off the table.

"Not with Mr. Hunt!" Esme clarified. "No, I mean . . . I saw the results from the Big Day. Do you have any idea how well you did? I thought we might start another club. Your list was so impressive, with all those females. They're much harder to spot, you know!"

"That's what I said!" Callie exclaimed, and Sid shushed her with a glance at Ben. "That's what I said!" Callie repeated in a whisper.

"Think about it," Esme said. "I'm not as expert as Mr. Hunt. But I'd be chuffed to host you in the library and learn with you."

"Only girls?" Callie asked.

"How about . . . anyone who's interested in a more inclusive sort of club?"

JOY McCULLOUGH

Callie looked to Sid, who nodded. Raj might want to stay with Mr. Hunt's club, if he was even welcome after reporting the club for cheating. He'd been in it a long time, and he was a serious twitcher. But if he didn't, he would be welcome in theirs. The old Callie would have been afraid to ask him, because he might say no. But this Callie knew it wouldn't be the end of the world if he did.

"What if . . . ?"

Esme grinned. "I'm almost guaranteed to say yes. What?"

"What if it's a Birds and Books club? I know you said a kids' book club might not take off, but what if we combine the two?"

"What, like books about birds?" Sid asked.

Callie shrugged. "Could be."

"Oh!" Esme yelped, and then clapped a hand over her mouth with a glance toward Ben. "*Call Me Alastair!* Or *The Someday Birds!* Or *One Came Home!*"

"It wouldn't have to be only books about birds," Callie said. "We could talk about books while we go on bird walks."

"I love it," Esme said.

"Sid? Are you okay?"

Sid's eyes had welled up with tears, which she hastily wiped away. "I've never been in one place long enough to belong to a club," she said. "At least not since my seizures started."

Callie reached out and grabbed Sid's hand. "You're here now. And you won't only be in this club. You'll be a founding member."

Ben wanted to get back to work right away, but Callie's parents said they'd fire him if he worked. They had plenty of other renovations to focus on; the landscaping could wait. When he began driving Sid absolutely bonkers, she begged them to let Ben get back to the work he could do from his chair—drafting garden plans and researching types of plants and placing orders.

With a new influx of money from the golf course developers, Callie's parents hired a team of young gardeners to do the physical work Ben couldn't. A couple of them were students at the high school. Callie watched them arrive each afternoon in their SKHS uniforms, disappear into a garden shed, and emerge in ratty jeans and T-shirts.

She passed them on the grounds sometimes, weeding flower beds or hauling rosebushes. They laughed and joked with one another, said hello to Callie, and once she heard them nervously encouraging one another to ask dates to an upcoming dance. They were a few years older than Callie, but they weren't a whole other species.

Ben walked the grounds slowly, overseeing his young charges. When he wasn't up to it, Sid took great delight in bossing the apprentice gardeners around. She always said Ben had told her to pass along the message. He usually hadn't.

Callie and Sid were walking with Ben one day almost a month after the heart attack when they reached the rounded stone wall they'd found during the birding Big Day.

"What's in here, Ben?" Callie asked. "Do you know?"

"Aye," he said. "It's a garden."

Sid looked around at the rolling hills and the blooming primroses and the swaying heather. "A garden in a garden?"

Ben smiled. "I believe this was Lady Whittington-Spence's rose garden."

"My parents mentioned that!" Callie said. "How do we get in? Can we?"

It looked like Mary Lennox's secret garden, encircled by tall stone walls and no sign of an entrance. Callie had grown to love the birds of the castle grounds, but she thought it unlikely one would suddenly swoop down and lead her to a hidden door.

As it happened, she didn't need a bird. "Over here, I believe." Ben walked them along the stone wall a ways until he stopped at a stretch that looked exactly like the rest of it. "Just need to clear these away," he said, beginning to pull at some vines.

"Stop that, Pops." Sid pulled her grandfather away, and she and Callie began to tug on the vines until finally the outline of a door became visible.

"Is there a key?"

"Nah," Ben said. "It's been open all along."

And it had. Callie had only to push on the door and it creaked, then swung all the way open to reveal a garden more beautiful than she could have imagined. It *was* like Mary Lennox's garden, all overgrown and wild, except not so abandoned. There were rosebushes everywhere, so many of them, and while tall grasses and weeds grew around them and vines covered the walls, the roses were blooming.

Ben sat down on a bench next to an enormous bush full of yellow blossoms. "I reckon Lady Philippa was caring for these right up until she died." He leaned in to take a deep sniff.

It was magical, like something out of a storybook, but it was also as real as the thorns snagging on Callie's jeans while she moved from rosebush to rosebush.

Up above, a bird called out. Callie froze. "Sid," she hissed. "Is that ... ?"

Sid stopped too. They both listened. It was familiar, but Callie couldn't quite place it until a black bird took off from a nearby tree and she spotted the red beak.

A red-billed chough. The first species they had seen together. The one Mr. Hunt had been so jealous of. This time there were no checklists or forms. It didn't matter if anyone else ever knew they'd seen this bird.

Callie and Sid both sat down on the stone bench on either side of Ben.

They sat, and they listened to the bird sing its song. Maybe it called out for its flock, like a starling, happiest with thousands of other birds. Or maybe it called out to its one mate, the one it needed to survive when food got scarce and temperatures dropped. Or maybe it simply sang, because it could, and it was beautiful.

May 12, 2021
South Kingsferry, Spence Castle

I hope you don't mind me writing in your
journal, Pippa. I like to think you left it for me
to find. Maybe not me, specifically, but that you
left it, hoping, knowing one day a girl would
find it. A girl who needed it. Who needed birds
like you did.

I found it.

And I found the birds.

Today I saw a red-billed chough. It lives
in the stone-walled rose garden. At least
I think it lives there. But it comes and
goes. To find food, or friends, or just to
fly because it can and wouldn't you fly, if
you could?

I don't really know why it leaves, or
why it comes back.

There's so much I don't know about
birds. It's kind of what I like about
them. I can spot them and record what I
see. Maybe I can identify their species.
But I can never know why some soar alone,
like herons, and some flock in massive
numbers, like starlings. I can never

know if a heron sometimes gets lonely, or a starling wishes for a moment of peace.

I'll never know, not really, what it's like to be drawn to migrate, pulled by an inexplicable inner compass toward that place I'll know as home the moment I land.

But I think maybe for me it's not the place so much as the others flying with me that tell me I'm home.

ACKNOWLEDGMENTS

When I was a toddler, my family moved to Scotland because my dad was getting his PhD at the University of Edinburgh. He struggled to find student housing for a family of four and had almost given up when he saw a small notice in the newspaper for a rental at Dundas Castle in South Queensferry. Which is how I ended up living in a Scottish castle for two years as a small child.

I was very young and have few memories of the time. But many thanks to my mom and dad and sister for sharing their memories, many of which made it into this book. (Looking at you, raven stuck in the chimney!)

Many thanks to my editor, Reka Simonsen, for taking

me under her wing. (I'm sorry, I had to.) Thank you also to her wonderful assistant Julia McCarthy, and to art director Greg Stadnyk and senior managing editor Jeannie Ng.

Romina Galotta created a cover more perfect than she could have known; when my mother saw it, she said that Callie looks just like I did as a child.

My agent, Jim McCarthy, is endlessly supportive, and I would be lost without him. Same goes for my critique partner, Jessica Lawson, who consulted on plot and character at a crucial stage.

I am indebted to the following people for their input on matters of Scottish language and culture, juvenile absence epilepsy, and Indian comfort food: Sophie Cameron, Susan Hancock, Jennifer and Joel Ziegler, and Rajani LaRocca. Any mistakes are my own.

I was so lucky to go to Scotland to research this book. Thank you to the staff at Dundas Castle for showing me around my former home!

And thank you as always to my family—Mariño, Cordelia, Joaquin—for always supporting me and my stories. I am so glad you are my murmuration of starlings.